The smell of blood had excited the big black and he was trembling. Throwing a leg over, Indian style, Mabry gave a piercing yell, and Healy slapped the horse across the haunches with his hat.

With a lunge, the black broke from the barn and Mabry fired from under the horse's neck, all in one swift motion. Barker broke for cover.

Slamming his heels into the black and yelling like a Comanche, Maby went after him. Barker turned as he ran and tried to bring his gun up fast, but it went off into the ground as the black hit him with a shoulder that knocked him reeling.

Barker fired from his knees, but the black reared then and the bullet only laid a hot lash along Mabry's cheek.

Then King Mabry fired three times as fast as he could slip the hammer off his thumb.

Barker backed up, swearing, and a stain spread on his shirt.

Mabry held his fire, waiting in silence as the wounded man struggled to lift his gun. Outside the barn, Healy and Janice stood frozen.

Barker's gun came up, then the muzzle tilted down and his eyes glazed over. He took two bent-kneed strides, and then he crumpled to the hard-packed earth.

King Mabry waited, eyes cold. Barker's body heaved at the waist, then slowly relaxed.

The wind rattled the cottonwood leaves. That was the only sound as Mabry reloaded.

Fawcett Gold Medal Books
by Louis L'Amour:

CROSSFIRE TRAIL

HELLER WITH A GUN

HONDO

KILKENNY

LAST STAND AT PAPAGO WELLS

SHOWDOWN AT YELLOW BUTTE

THE TALL STRANGER

TO TAME A LAND

UTAH BLAINE

# HELLER
# WITH A GUN

by
Louis L'Amour

Fawcett Gold Medal • New York

# HELLER
# WITH A GUN

# HELLER
# WITH A GUN

## Chapter One

HE WAS RIDING southwest in a gathering storm and behind him a lone man clung to his trail.

It was bitter cold. . . .

He came down off the ridge into the shelter of the draw with the wind kicking up snow behind him. The sky was a flat slate gray, unbroken and low. The air grew colder by the minute and there was a savage bite to the wind.

He was a big, wide-shouldered man with a lean, strong-boned face. His black, flat-crowned hat was pulled low, the collar of his sheep-lined coat turned up. Wind-whipped particles of snow rattled off his coat like thrown gravel.

He was two days out of Deadwood and riding for Cheyenne, and the nearest shelter was at Hat Creek Station, probably fifty miles along.

Wind knifed at his exposed cheek. He drew deeply on his cigarette. Whoever followed him had the same problem. Find shelter or die. The wind was a moving wall of snow and the evening was filled with vast sound.

There is something fiercely insensate about a Wyoming or Dakota blizzard, something malevolent and shocking in its brutality. It ripped at him now, smashing him with jarring fists of wind, and raking his face with claws of blown ice.

King Mabry lowered his head to shield his face, breathing with his mouth open. Whenever he lifted his head the wind whipped at him, sucking air from his lungs.

When they came to the creek bottom it was suddenly. The horse plunged belly-deep in the snow and began fighting for a foothold. Forcing the black through a crackle of frozen brush, he let it slide and stumble to the creek bottom.

Here was respite from the wind. The creek was narrow, sheathed in ice, yet the high banks and the trees offered protection. He headed downstream.

It was bitter cold. . . .

When he found what he wanted it was more than he expected. The creek turned a rocky shoulder and had heaved some logs and brush over a triangle of huge boulders. On the downstream side there was an opening. When he had pulled the brush away he had a cave fifteen feet deep and almost seven feet high.

Leading the horse inside, Mabry began to work swiftly. He cut evergreens and made a windbreak that could be shifted if the wind changed, and which would also serve to reflect the heat from his fire back into the cave.

With shredded bark from the underside of a log, some dry leaves from the same place, and some twigs broken from the trunks of trees, he built a fire. He added fuel and the blaze mounted higher.

There was no shortage of fuel, yet he dragged several dead branches closer, and one half-rotted log. Stumbling through deepening snow, he cut evergreen boughs for a bed. Heat from the fire and the warmth of the horse's body would make the shelter warm enough for survival, if no more.

Working slowly, he rubbed the horse down, then hung half his supply of corn over the horse's nose in its feed bag.

The great stones warmed slowly, gathering heat from

the fire. Outside the wind howled. His thoughts turned to the man who followed him.

Somehow he must have learned of the money Mabry was carrying. Several hundred dollars of his own money, and a thousand dollars to be returned to the rancher in Cheyenne.

The trouble was that when a man had a reputation as a gun fighter, somebody always believed his gun was for hire.

The trouble was that in a time and area when all men carried guns, and used them on occasion, he used them too well.

He had given it no thought until that bright morning when he was sixteen, and he rode into the Cup on the old XIT with Bent Forrest.

Two rustlers had a steer down and a hot iron. The rustlers saw them first and the nearest man had a gun lifting when Mabry drew. He was sixteen then, and nobody in the outfit knew anything about him except that he worked hard and talked little. A moment later they started to learn.

Bent Forrest was a gun-handy man, but on that morning both men were down and kicking before his gun cleared leather. He looked from them to the kid and his throat worked.

"You ever kill a man before?"

"No."

They sat their horses in the morning sunlight while the branding fire smoldered and the steer struggled helplessly. The two rustlers lay sprawled, their guns flung free in that last moment when death came sharply.

"You'll have to take it easy, kid. You're good. Maybe the best I've seen."

King Mabry looked at the dead men on the ground. Wind stirred the handkerchief tied to the nearest man's neck. Mabry felt sick and empty and lost.

"It was them or us, kid. We'll say nothing about this."

Then one night when drinking, Forrest bragged. He knew what a reputation as a gun fighter could do to a man, but he was drinking and he bragged. A tough puncher from down on the Pecos started hunting the kid to prove Forrest wrong.

They buried the tough puncher on a windy hilltop near old Tascosa, where he could lie beside Frank Valley and the boys who died in the Big Fight. And King Mabry drifted.

Fort Stockton, Lampasas, Mobeetie, Uvalde. The Big Bend, El Paso, Lincoln, Cimarron. North and west with trail herds to Kansas, to Nebraska and Wyoming.

From time to time he had to use his gun. . . .

He awakened in the first cold light of dawn. He lunged from his blankets and stirred the remains of his fire. He tossed on some dry leaves, some bark, and a piece of evergreen bough. Then he scrambled back into his bed, shaking with cold.

It was far below zero. He knew by the wind, by the pistol crack of frozen branches, by the crisp sharpness of the air.

After an interminable time a faint tendril of smoke lifted, a tiny flame appeared, and the pine needles flared hotly. He thrust an arm from under the blankets and tossed more fuel into the fire.

When he could feel the warmth in the shelter, he got up and dressed quickly, then shouldered into his sheepskin. He drew one gun from its holster, checked it, and thrust it behind his belt.

With a friendly slap on the black's rump he stepped past the horse and stood beside the windbreak, looking out into the morning.

He faced downstream. Occasionally the white veil of falling or blown snow would break and he could see as far as the point, some thirty yards away. Flakes touched his cheek with damp fingers. He narrowed his eyes, studying what lay outside.

Mabry was not a trusting man. The facts of his life

had left no room for trust. In the hard years following that morning on the XIT he learned his lesson well, and learned the hard way. His eyes went to that point of trees around which the stream bent in a slow arc. He studied them, started to step outside, and then he stopped.

Mabry did not know why he hesitated.

A gust whipped snow into the air, lashing at his face, sucking at his lungs. And a man's subconscious can be his best friend.

Mabry stood very still.

He was invisible from the outside. Another step and he would be framed black against the snow.

A hunter can walk in the forest when the wind blows with its many sounds, yet if a rabbit moves in the brush his ears recognize the sound. Upon the vast plain or the desert the flight of a buzzard may pass unnoticed, for the buzzard belongs to the landscape. The cacti form weird shapes, the ocotillo carries a miniature forest of lances, yet if a rider moves upon that desert he will be seen.

The hunter and the hunted . . . these two are kin. Their senses are alert to the same stimuli, awaken to the same far-off sounds. A shadow in the wrong place, a flicker of sun reflection, a creak of leather . . . each may be a warning.

And for these things and a thousand others the senses of hunter and hunted are alert. Often the exact warning is not recognized; it is a subconscious perception.

So King Mabry now waited for the snow veil to break once more. He had learned to trust his instincts. Attention might lag, reason might fail, but the instincts were first born and would be the last to die.

The snow was unbroken. No tracks were anywhere visible. On the point the trees grew close, their boughs interlaced and thickly mingled with a darker bulk of pines. All were heavy with snow.

Mabry rolled a smoke and lighted it. Something was wrong out there and he did not intend to move until he knew what it was. In his lifetime he had known a few reckless men, a few who tried to be daring, who took unnecessary risks to show what they believed to be courage. He had helped to bury them.

He was playing a game where life was the blue chip. A step into the open meant to chuck that blue chip on the table. And he had but one.

His eyes returned to the trees.

He thrust his right hand into the front of his coat to warm his fingers against his body. Stiff fingers might fumble or drop a gun.

Then his eyes saw what his brain knew was there: a spot of darkness in the tops of the trees.

A small thing, a simple thing, yet the price of a man's life. A place in the branches where there was no snow.

Somebody had to be under that spot with a going fire. Rising heat waves had melted the snow above it.

It was all of thirty yards away, but knowing now where he must look, King Mabry found it.

Drifted snow over a pile of debris. Not so large or imposing as his own shelter, but enough to conceal a man who lay in warmth while he waited with a rifle for Mabry to emerge and die.

Mabry possessed one advantage. His pursuer could not be aware that his presence was known. From behind the windbreak Mabry studied the situation with infinite care.

The unknown watcher lay close to the ground, which decreased his field of vision. Without rising from his hiding place that man could see nothing lower than three feet above the ground, and the snow was that deep in the creek bottom.

Dropping to his knees, Mabry dug out snow, working with care to disturb no snow where it might be seen by the watcher. He worked slowly. In that temperature perspiration could easily be fatal, for when one stopped working the moisture would freeze into a thin film of ice inside one's clothing, and death would follow quickly.

There was a huge log, a great snow-covered tree that

lay on an angle, its far end almost flanking the hiding place of the watcher. Mabry dug his way to that deadfall, then crawled along the ground behind it. When he reached the upthrust roots at its base, he stood up.

Concealed by the wall of tangled roots and frozen earth embedded around them, he could see behind the shelter, yet at first he saw nothing.

A snowflake touched his cheek with a damp, cold finger. Mabry brushed his coat. Wind picked up a flurry of snow, swept it along, then allowed it to settle down. The wind was not blowing so hard now. A branch cracked in the cold. There was no other sound but the wind.

Smoke rose from his own fire, and a thin tendril of smoke that died quickly from the watcher's shelter.

Mabry kept his right hand under his coat and close to his gun. He was forty yards away. Slow anger was building in him. He did not like to be hunted. Whoever the watcher was, he planned murder.

Mabry's face, darkened by many suns and winds, seemed now to be drawn in hard planes. It was a still face, remote, lonely. It was the face of a hunter.

He did not want to kill, yet he did not want to die. And this man had chosen the field, selected his victim. Yet he did not know the manner of man he hunted. He looked for a fat cat, he found a tiger.

Wind flurried. Behind the shelter there was an indefinite movement.

He felt the cold, knew he could not long remain away from his fire. Yet this was the time for decision.

He was born to the gun. He had lived by the gun. Perhaps someday he would die by the gun. He had not chosen the way, but it was his way and he lived among men who often understood no other.

Mabry could be patient now. He knew what lay ahead, knew what he could do. He had been hunted before, by Kiowas, Comanches, Sioux, and Apaches. He had also been hunted by his own kind.

He took his hand from his coat and rolled a smoke.

He put it in his lips and lit up. He squinted his eyes against the first exhalation and looked past the blown smoke at the shelter. He warmed away the momentary chill that had come to his hand.

There was no target, nothing. The man there was warm. He was cold. There was no sense in waiting longer.

A heavy branch of evergreen hung over the other man's shelter, thick with a weight of snow, a bit away from the circle of warmth from the fire . . . but near enough.

Mabry drew his gun, tested the balance in his palm, judged the distance, and fired.

Cut by the bullet, the branch broke and the snow fell, partly outside the shelter, partly inside. And probably on the man's fire.

The sound of the shot racketed down the ravine, and silence followed.

Mabry's feet were icy. The chill was beginning to penetrate. He thrust his gun back inside his coat and watched a little smoke rise, thick smoke.

The hidden man had lost his fire.

The slide of snow from the branch had done what Mabry hoped it would, and now the watcher must lie there in the cold to await death by freezing, or he must come out.

Yet Mabry himself was cold, and the hidden man had shelter from the wind.

A slight movement within the shelter alerted him, but nobody appeared. The watcher's shelter was only a place where a man could keep from the wind. There was no room for fuel, scarcely space for a man and a fire.

Wind whined among the trees. Branches creaked in the cold. Snow flurried, whipped across the point, then died out. The wind was going down, the storm was over. Yet Mabry did not intend to be followed when he moved on again.

He moved quickly to another hiding place behind a

tree. He was not twenty yards from the man's hideout now and he could see the darkness of the hole into which the man had crawled.

This man had waited in ambush to kill him. He had followed him for two days or more.

"Come out."

Mabry did not speak loudly, for in the still air the smallest sound could be heard. "Come out with your hands up, or come shootin'."

Silence. . . .

And then he came with a lunge, throwing himself from the shelter, rifle in hand. He had heard Mabry's voice, so he knew where to look, yet the instant it took to separate his target from the trunks of the trees was fatal.

Yet at the last moment, Mabry shot high. His bullet smashed the man on the shoulder, turning him half around. The rifle dropped and the wounded man grasped at the wound, going to his knees in the snow. Then he fell, grabbing for the rifle.

King Mabry balanced his gun in his palm and walked nearer, ready to fire. He was cursing himself for a fool for not shooting to kill, yet in the instant he glimpsed the man's face, he knew this was no gunman. And why add even a coyote to his list of killings?

Get me killed someday, he told himself cynically.

The wounded man had fallen against the front of his shelter, which was only a hollow under the roots of a blow-down. There was blood on the snow, and blood on the man's shoulder and chest.

He stared up at Mabry, hating him. He was a sallow-faced man with lean cheeks and a hawk's hard face and a scar over one eye. Now it was a frightened face, but not one Mabry had ever seen before.

"You . . . you goin' to stand there?"

"Why not?" Mabry asked coldly. "I wasn't huntin' you."

"I hope you die! I hope you die hard!"

"I will," Mabry said. "I've been expecting it for years. Who put you on me?"

"Why tell you?" the man sneered.

"You can tell me," Mabry said without emotion, "or you can die there in the snow."

Grudgingly the wounded man said, "It was Hunter. If you didn't take the job, you were to die."

Mabry understood the truth of that. Ever since he arrived in Deadwood and understood why he had been hired, he should have expected this. They could not afford to have him talk.

No man lost blood in such cold and lasted long without care. If he left this man, he would die. Dropping to his knee, he reached for the shoulder. The fellow grabbed at Mabry's gun and Mabry hit him with his fist. Then he bound up the wound with makeshifts and then gathered up the guns and walked back to his own shelter. He had planned to stay another night, but there was evidence that the storm was breaking, and regardless of that, he could not keep the man here or leave him to die.

He rolled his bed and saddled up, then drank the rest of the coffee.

Mounting, he rode back to where the man lay. The fellow was conscious, but he looked bad.

"Where's your horse?"

Too weak to fight, the man whispered an answer, and Mabry rode to the clay bank behind some trees, where he found a beat-up buckskin, more dead than alive.

Mabry saddled him after brushing off the snow and rubbing some semblance of life into the horse with a handful of rough brown grass.

When he got back to the man's shelter he picked the fellow up and shook him. "Get up on that horse," he said. "We'll start for Hat Creek. Make a wrong move and I'll blow you out of the saddle."

He took the blankets and threw them around the man to keep in what warmth his body could develop.

It would be cold tonight, but with luck he could make Hat Creek Station.

Wind flapped his hat brim and snow sifted across the trail. He lifted the black into a trot. The country about them was white and still. In the distance he could see a line of trees along another creek.

His mind was empty. He did not think. Only the occasional tug on the lead rope reminded him of the man who rode behind him.

It was a hard land, and it bred hard men to hard ways.

## Chapter Two

KING MABRY followed Old Woman Creek to Hat Creek Station in the last cold hour of a bitterly cold day.

Under the leafless cottonwoods whose bare branches creaked with cold he drew rein. His breath clouded in the cold air, and as his eyes took in the situation his fingers plucked absently at the thin ice that had accumulated on his scarf.

He was a man who never rode without caution, never approached a strange place without care.

There were no tracks but those from the station to the barn. There was no evidence of activity but the slow smoke rising from the chimney.

One thing was unexpected. Drawn alongside the barn were two large vans, and beneath the coating of frost bright-colored lettering was visible. He could not, at this distance, make out the words.

Nobody emerged as he approached the station. No door opened. There was no sign of welcome.

Everything was still in the bitter evening cold; even the rising smoke seemed stiff in the unfamiliar air.

Hat Creek Station had originally been built by soldiers sent to establish a post on Hat Creek in Nebraska. Unfamiliar with the country, they had crossed into Wyoming and built on Sage Creek. When abandoned by the Army, it became a stage station on the route from Cheyenne to Black Hills, and a post office. From the beginning its history had been wild and bloody.

Mabry knew the stories. They had come down the trails as all such stories did, from campfire to card table, from bunkhouse to chuck wagon.

It was at Hat Creek that Stutterin' Brown, a stage-company man, emerged second best from a pistol argument with Persimmons Bill over stolen horses. They buried Brown.

A party of freighters bound for the Black Hills was attacked by several hundred Indians near Hat Creek Station, and was saved only by the arrival of a troop of cavalry from Rawhide Buttes.

Near a place known locally as Robbers' Roost, a few miles from the station, there had been a series of holdups, and it was near there that Boone May, a shotgun guard, killed an outlaw.

Hat Creek Station was a convenient wayside stop for travelers from Cheyenne to Black Hills, and at one time or another most of the noted characters and gun fighters of the West had passed through.

It was here that Calamity Jane was fired from her job as a government packer, for drunkenness. And here, at various times, had stopped such men as Wild Bill Hickok, Wyatt Earp, Sam Bass, Joel Collins, Scott Davis, Seth Bullock, Big-Nose George, and Lame Bradley.

In short, the patrons of Hat Creek Station were men with the bark on.

Swinging around the barn to the door, Mabry stepped from the saddle, pulled the pin from the latch, and, swinging wide the door, herded the two horses in ahead of him. Then he pulled the door shut and fastened it securely.

Standing behind his horse, he remained there until his eyes grew accustomed to the dimness within the vast barn. When he could see again, he located an unoccupied stall and stripped the saddle and bridle from the black.

Then he untied the wounded man from the saddle of the buckskin and helped him to the ground.

The man wilted then, scarcely able to keep his legs under him.

"Can you walk?"

The man looked at him sullenly. "I can walk."

"Then you're on your own. You cross my trail again and I'll finish the job."

The man turned and staggered to the door, almost fell there, but caught at the door to hold his balance. Then he pushed it open and walked out into the snow.

Mabry turned back to his horse and carefully rubbed him down, working over him patiently and with care.

Somewhere a door closed and Mabry heard a man coming down the wide aisle between the two rows of stalls.

The hostler was a tall man with an unusually small face, very round and clean shaved.

He halted, staring into the darkness of the stall where Mabry worked.

"Come far?"

"No."

The hostler puffed on his pipe. He had never seen this man before and it was indiscreet to ask questions, but the hostler was a curious man—and he knew that beat-up buckskin.

He gestured. "Ain't in good shape."

"Better shape than the man who rode him."

Griffin, the hostler remembered, was considered a very salty customer in some circles. He must have cut himself into the wrong circle.

"He has friends."

"You?"

"Shuckins, man. I'm just hostler here. Knowed Pete, like most folks."

Mabry had removed the scarf from around his hat and the sheepskin coat hung open. The hostler had seen the guns.

"Admire to know what happened."

Mabry picked up his rifle and saddlebags with his left hand. He did not exactly gesture, but the hostler decided not to leave any room for doubt. He preceded Mabry to the door.

When they reached it, Mabry said, "He laid for me."

The hostler had suspected for a long time that Griffin was one of that crowd. Knew it, in fact, without having a particle of information. So he laid for the wrong man.

Mabry stepped out into the cold. The thermometer beside the door read forty degrees below zero.

"Man around called Benton. Him an' Joe Noss. They're partial to Pete Griffin."

"Thanks."

Snow crunched under his boots as he crossed to the station and lifted the latch. He pushed open the door and stepped into the hot, smoke-filled air of the room.

There was a smell of rank tobacco and drying wool, a shuffling of feet and a riffling of cards. The potbellied stove glowed with heat and five men sat around a table playing poker with several onlookers. All the seated men had removed their coats. They wore wool shirts and suspenders.

From an adjoining room there was a rattle of dishes, and Mabry saw another door that led off to the left of the bar. He remained where he was, taking time to study the occupants of the room. His open coat revealed the guns, and he wore no glove on his right hand.

Somebody coughed and somebody else said, "I'll take three cards." Chips clicked, feet shuffled.

Alone at the bar was a man who wore a cloth coat, narrow at the waist with a wide fur collar. He had a round fur cap on his head, the earlaps turned up and tied on top. He glanced at Mabry, frankly curious.

There was nobody in the room that Mabry knew until the bartender turned around.

Mabry crossed to the bar and put his saddlebags on top, leaning the Winchester against the bar.

The bartender's face was flushed. He glanced quickly, guiltily around, then touched his lips with his tongue. He was obviously worried and nervous.

" 'Lo, King. I—"

Something that might have been amusement flickered

briefly in the big man's eyes. He stared gravely at the bartender. "Know your face, but . . . What was that name again?"

"Williams." The man spoke hastily, his relief obvious. "Bill Williams."

"Sure. Sorry I forgot."

The bartender ducked below bar level and came up with a square, dusty bottle. "Little o' the Irish. On the house."

Mabry accepted the bottle without comment and filled a glass. He lifted it, sighting through the amber whisky to catch the light.

"Has the smell o' the peat, that Irish does."

Mabry glanced briefly at the man in the fur-collared coat, then pushed the bottle toward him.

"The name's Healy. Tom Healy, of the Healy Traveling Shows." He lifted the whisky, treasuring it in his hand. "The best they'd offer me was barrel whisky."

They drank, replacing their glasses on the bar. Mabry let his eyes canvass the room, probing for possible trouble. A man remained alive by knowing what to expect and what direction to expect it from. And there was a man near the card table with a long, narrow face filled with latent viciousness. He stood near a slack-jawed man with shifty eyes.

The man in the fur-collared coat spun a gold coin on the bar and refilled their glasses.

In the momentary stillness of the room the sound of the coin was distinct and clear. Heads turned and eyes held on the coin, then lifted to the face of the man in the fur collar. An Eastern face, an Eastern man, a tenderfoot. And then their eyes went naturally to Mabry, and seemed to pause.

"Easy with that gold, mister." Mabry lifted his glass. "Maybe half the men in this room would slit your throat for it."

Healy's smile was friendly, yet faintly taunting. "I'm green, friend, but not that green. Even if I'm Irish."

Mabry tossed off the whisky. "You fork your own broncs in this country," he said, and turned abruptly away.

He took up his rifle and saddlebags and stepped out toward the adjoining room, and then he missed a stride and almost stopped, for a girl had just come into the room.

She walked with quick, purposeful steps, but as their eyes met her step faltered, too. Then she caught herself and went on by, leaving him with a flashing memory of red-gold hair and a gray traveling dress whose like he had not seen since Richmond. He opened the inner door and entered the hallway beyond. Away from the fire, it was cold.

Along the hall on one side were four doors. These he surmised led to separate rooms. On the left side was one door, which he opened. This led to a long room lined with tiers of bunks, three high. The room would sleep thirty. Choosing an empty bunk near the door, he dumped his gear.

He shucked his sheepskin coat, then his belt and gun. The second gun stayed in his waistband.

City girl . . . must be with the Healy show. Her eyes had looked into his, straight and clean. Not boldly, but with assurance and self-possession. She was all woman, that one. And a lady.

None of his affair.

His thoughts reverted to the men in the room. Dispassionately, yet with knowledge born of long experience, he could see what would happen. Within thirty minutes or less Griffin's friends would know he had come in and under what circumstances. What happened then would depend on how far they would go for a friend.

Not far . . . unless it would serve their own ends, or one of them was building a reputation.

Or unless the man with the narrow face was one of them. That one had a devil riding him. He would kill.

If the weather broke by daybreak he would push on. He took the gun from his waistband and spun the cylinder. It was a solid, well-made gun. He returned it to his belt and walked back to the outer room.

"How about grub?"

Williams jerked his head toward an open door through which came the rattle of dishes. "Beef and beans, maybe more. Best cook this side of the IXL in Deadwood."

Mabry walked around the bar into a long room with two tables placed end to end. Benches lined either side. At the far end of the table near the fireplace Healy sat with the girl, and with a big man whom Mabry had not seen before.

He was a man with a wide face and a geniality that immediately rubbed Mabry the wrong way. Better dressed than most of the men in the outer room, he held a fat black cigar between his fingers.

"Take some doing, all right. But we can do it."

The big man was speaking. He glanced down the table at Mabry, who was helping himself to dishes that an aproned man had put before him. The big man lowered his voice, but it was still loud enough for Mabry to hear.

"West out of here into the Wind River country. Then north. There'll be fuel along the Big Horn."

"What about Indians?"

The big man waved his cigar. "No trouble. Mostly Shoshones up thataway, and they're friendly."

Healy made no comment, but he glanced at Mabry, who was eating in silence. Healy seemed about to speak, but changed his mind. Twice the girl looked at Mabry, and he was aware of her glance.

The fellow was either a fool or a liar. Going up that valley was tough at any time, but in the dead of winter, with a woman along, it was asking for trouble. And with two loaded vans. As for Indians, the Shoshones were friendly, but there were roving bands of renegade Sioux who had taken to the rough country after the Custer fight and had never returned to the reservation. Only last week a couple of trappers out of Spearfish had been murdered up in the Big Horns. Their companions found their bodies and plenty of Indian sign. They lit out for Deadwood and the story had been familiar around town before Mabry took the outtrail. It was not the only case. Mabry had talked to them, had bought the black horse from them, in fact.

"I'll have my two men," the big man said. "That will make four of us and the three women."

Three women. . . .

And those renegade Sioux did not have their squaws with them.

He filled his cup and put the coffeepot down. The girl glanced around and for an instant their eyes held, then she looked away.

"Join us, friend?" Healy suggested.

"Thanks," Mabry said. "I don't want to interrupt."

It was obvious that the big man was not pleased at the invitation. He was irritated, and shifted angrily on the bench.

"We're planning a trip," Healy said. "You can help."

Only the irritation of the big man prompted him. Otherwise he would have stayed where he was. He shifted his food up the table and sat facing the big man and the girl.

"King," Healy said, "meet Janice Ryan. She's with my troupe. And this is Andy Barker, who's agreed to guide us to Alder Gulch."

"In this weather?"

Barker's face tightened. "I told them it wouldn't be easy, but I know that trail." He hesitated, then took a chance. "Do you?"

"No."

Barker showed his relief. "Then I'm afraid you won't be much use to us," he said abruptly, "but thanks, anyway."

"I haven't been over that trail, but I've been over a lot of others in bad weather."

Barker brushed the ash from his cigar, ignoring Mabry. "That's about it. We can leave as soon as the weather breaks."

"You missed your count," Healy said. "There'll be another man."

Baker looked quickly at Mabry. "You?" Obviously the idea was distasteful to him.

"No," Healy said, "although we'd like to have him. I referred to the other man in our company, Doc Guilford."

"Oh. . . . All right."

Mabry tried his coffee and found it hot and strong. The room was very still. On the hearth the fire crackled briefly, then subsided. Barker drew on his cigar, seeming to want to leave, but hesitating, as if he disliked leaving them alone to talk to Mabry.

Or was that, Mabry asked himself, his imagination? He might be letting an irrational dislike of the man influence his judgment. Mabry liked the coffee, and it warmed away the last of his chill. He liked sitting across the table from Janice Ryan and could feel the sharp edge of her curiosity.

"Take quite a while, a trip like that," he ventured. "Better have plenty of grub and some spare horses."

"When we want your advice," Barker said, "we'll ask for it."

King Mabry lifted his eyes. He looked at Barker for a long time, then said quietly, "I've been asked," he reminded him, "by him." He indicated Healy. "Or do you have some reason for not wanting them to get advice from anyone else?"

Barker stared at him, his lips tightening. He was about to speak when Williams came into the room.

"Mabry," he said quickly in a low tone, "watch yourself. Trouble making up."

"Thanks."

He saw startled comprehension in Barker's eyes and saw the man grow faintly white around the eyes as he heard Mabry's name.

Trouble might mean that Griffin's friends were going to take action. That could mean nothing to Barker, but the name obviously had. It had proved a severe jolt, by the look of him.

"King . . . King Mabry."

"That's the name."

Barker smiled stiffly. "Healy," he said, "when you introduce a man, use his whole name. It might make a difference."

"The bartender called him King. It was the only name I knew."

"Does it matter so much?" Janice asked.

"In this case, yes." Barker chose his words with care, yet they carried the information he intended, and a warning. "King Mabry is a known man. They say he has killed fifteen men."

Mabry's eyes were bleak. He gave Barker all his attention. "Not fifteen. Only eleven—not counting Indians."

Barker got up, smiling faintly, obviously feeling he had scored a point against Mabry. Yet as he turned to go, King Mabry spoke. The remark came from nowhere, unconsidered, unplanned. "One thing, Barker. They were all armed, and they were all facing me."

The big man stiffened, and the glance he threw over his shoulder at Mabry was malignant. Yet it held a probing, half-frightened curiosity, too.

As he watched the man leave, Mabry's mind caught at that final reaction. Somewhere, Mabry told himself, he's shot a man in the back, or been accused of it.

It was something to remember. Something not to forget. Nor was Barker an enemy to be underrated. The big man was too confident not to have victory behind him. He was no fool. He was a shrewd, tough, dangerous man.

There was an uncomfortable silence in the room after Andy Barker had gone. Mabry drank his coffee and refilled the cup.

"None of my business," he said, "but I'd think about that trip. You'll have trouble."

Healy shifted his cup on his saucer and said nothing. Janice Ryan started to speak, then stopped. Silence stretched taut between the walls, and then a board creaked, and when they looked around a man was standing in the door.

He was a tall man, somewhat stooped, with a lean hatchet face, and he wore his gun tied down. And King Mabry knew the kind of man he was, and what to expect.

Low-voiced, he said, "Better get out. This is real trouble. Gun trouble."

## Chapter Three

NOBODY MOVED. The man in the doorway looked down the table at Mabry, then advanced a step into the room. When he stopped his right side was toward them.

His features were lean and vulpine. Mabry could see that the fellow was primed for a killing, and he was the man he had seen watching the game in the outer room.

"You brought in Pete Griffin?"

Mabry's right side was toward the door as he sat on the bench. His coffee cup, freshly filled, was before him. He waited while a slow count of five might have been made, and then he replied, "I brought him in."

"Where's Pete now?"

The speaker came on another step, his eyes holding on Mabry.

"I said, where's Pete?"

"Heard you." Mabry looked around at him. "You want him, go find him."

A second man came into the room and moved wide of the first. This man was not hunting trouble. "Bent?"

Benton ignored him. He had come into the room set for a killing, for a quick flare of anger, then shooting. Yet the attitude of Mabry gave him nothing upon which to hang it.

Mabry took the cup and cradled it in his hands. Benton tensed; Mabry might throw the hot coffee. He drew back half a step.

Healy looked from Mabry to Benton, seemingly aware for the first time that the situation was taut with danger. Sweat began to bead his brow, and his lips tightened. There was only one door and Benton stood with his back to it. Janice Ryan sat very still, her attention centered on Mabry.

27

"Bent?"

Distracted, Benton turned a little. "Shut up!"

Aware of his mistake, he jerked back, but Mabry seemed oblivious even of his presence. Mabry tasted his coffee. Then, putting down the cup, he fished in his shirt pocket for makings and began to build a smoke.

"Bent," the smaller man persisted, "not now. This ain't the place."

Benton was himself unsure. Mabry's failure to react to his challenge upset him. He dared not draw and shoot a man in the presence of witnesses when the man made no overt move, and when, as far as he could see, the man was not even wearing a gun.

Yet he could see no way to let go and get out. He hesitated, then repeated, "I want to know where Griffin is!"

Mabry struck a match and lit his cigarette.

Benton's face flushed. He considered himself a dangerous man and was so considered by others. Yet Mabry did not seem even to take him seriously.

"By God!" He took an angry step forward. "If you've killed Pete—"

Mabry looked around at him. "Why don't you get out of here?"

His tone was bored, slightly tinged with impatience.

Benton's resentment burst into fury and his right hand dropped to his gun.

Yet as his hand dropped, Mabry's right slapped back and grabbed Benton's wrist, spinning him forward and off balance. Instantly Mabry swung both feet over the bench and smashed into the man before he could regain his balance.

Knocked against the wall, his breath smashed from him, Benton tried to turn and draw, but as he turned, Mabry hit him with a wicked right to the chin that completed the turn for him. And as it ended, Mabry swung an underhanded left to the stomach.

Benton caught the punch in the solar plexus and it jerked his mouth open as he gasped for wind. Mabry hit him with a right, then a left that knocked him against the wall again, and a right that bounced his skull hard off the wall. The gunman slumped to the floor.

King Mabry turned on the smaller man. "You'll be Joe Noss. You wanted out of this, so you're out. But take him with you."

And as the white-faced Noss stooped to get hold of Benton, Mabry added, "And both of you stay out of my way."

He sat down and picked up his cigarette. He drew deep, and as his eyes met Janice's he said, "If that's too brutal, better get out. It's nothing to what you're liable to see between here and Alder Gulch."

"I didn't say anything," she said. "I didn't say anything at all."

He got up abruptly, irritated with himself. He was no kid to be upset by the first pretty girl who came along. He had seen a lot of women, known a lot of them.

But not like this one. Never like this one.

He walked out and nobody said anything. At the bar he stopped, aware of the undercurrent of interest. Hat Creek Station had seen much rough, brutal action, but fists were not much used where guns were carried. It was something new to be considered in estimating the caliber of King Mabry.

No place for a woman, Mabry told himself.

Behind him the momentary silence held. Then Tom Healy looked at Janice. "I'm a fool. You shouldn't be out here. None of you should."

"Because of that? That could happen anywhere."

"It may be worse. That's what he said."

She looked across the table, knowing what this trip meant to Healy, knowing there was nothing back East for him.

"Do you want to quit, Tom? Is that it?"

"You know me better than that."

"All right, then. We'll go on."

"There's only trails. We may run short of supplies before we get through. And there's Indians."

"Friendly Indians."

"You've a choice. I haven't. I failed back East. I'm bankrupt. The frontier's my last chance."

She looked at him, her eyes grave and quiet. "It may be that for a lot of us, Tom."

His coffee was cold, so he took another cup and filled it. He had no idea why Janice was willing to go West with him. Maybe somewhere back along the line of days she had known her own failure. Nevertheless, what he had said was true. For him there was no turning back. He had to make it on the frontier or he was through.

He had been finished when the letter from Jack Langrishe reached him, telling of the rich harvest to be reaped on the frontier in the cow and mining towns. Langrishe had a theatre in Deadwood, and there were other places. So Tom Healy put together his little troupe of five people and started West.

He had not been good enough for New York and Philadelphia. He had not been good enough for London, either. Not to be at the top, and that was where he wanted to be.

The Western trip began well. They made expenses in St. Louis and Kansas City. They showed a profit in Caldwell, Newton, and Ellsworth. In Dodge and Abilene they did better, but in Cheyenne they found the competition of a better troupe and barely broke even. And the other troupe was going on West.

Then Healy heard about Alder Gulch. For ten years it had been a boom camp. Now it was tapering off. The big attractions missed it now, yet there was still money there, and they wanted entertainment.

It was winter and the snow was two feet deep on the level, except where the fierce winds had blown the ground free. Alder Gulch was far away in Montana, but with luck and Barker to guide them, they could get through. Yet Mabry's doubt worried him. He was a good judge of people, and Mabry was a man who should know. And he did not seem to be a man to waste breath on idle talk.

Yet what else to do?

The ground had been free of snow when they left Cheyenne, the weather mild for the time of year. Hat Creek Station had been the first stop on the northward trek. And they were snowed in.

It was part of his profession to put up a front, and being an Irishman, he did it well. Actually, there was less than a thousand dollars of his own money in the ironbound box. There was that much more that belonged to the others, and—something that nobody knew but himself—there was also fifteen thousand dollars in gold that he was taking to Maguire in Butte to build a theatre.

Secretly he admitted to himself that he headed a company of misfits. Janice was no actress. She was a beautiful girl who should be married to some man of wealth and position. She had spoken to him vaguely of past theatrical successes, but he knew they were the sort of lie the theatre breeds. What actor or actress was ever strictly honest about past successes or failures? Certainly not Tom Healy. And certainly not that charming old windbag, Doc Guilford.

Janice was not even the type. She was competent, he admitted that, and on the frontier all they demanded was a woman. If she was pretty, so much the better.

Janice had that scarcely definable something that indicates breeding. Tom Healy was Irish, and an Irishman knows a thoroughbred. But like them all, Janice was running from something. Probably only fear of poverty among her own kind.

Doc Guilford was an old fraud. But an amusing fraud with a variety of talents, and he could be funny.

Of them all, Maggie had been the best. Maggie had gone up, partly on talent, partly on beauty. Her mistake was to love the theatre too much, and she stayed with it. Her beauty faded, but she still kept on . . . and she would always keep on.

How old was Maggie? Fifty? Or nearer sixty? Or only a rough-weather forty-five?

She had rheumatism and she complained about the rough riding of the wagons, but on stage her old tear-jerkers could still reach any crowd she played to. And in her dramatic roles she was always good.

Of them all, Dodie Saxon was the only one who might be on the way up. She was seventeen, eighteen, or nineteen. Nobody knew, and Dodie was not talking. She was tall and she was well built and she was sexy. She could dance and she could sing, and, moreover, she was a solid citizen. She was a clear-thinking youngster with both feet on the ground, and of them all, she was the only one with a future.

And these were the people he was taking off into the middle of a Wyoming winter over a trail he had never seen, into a country where he would be completely out of place.

The only shooting he had ever done was in a shooting gallery, and he had never killed so much as a rabbit or slept out of doors even one night.

Until he was eleven he had lived in a thatched hut in Ireland, then on a back street in Dublin, and after that he had never been far from a theatre or rooming house. When he had money he ordered meals; when he had no money he starved. But he had never cooked a meal in his life.

So it was Alder Gulch or break up the company and turn them loose to sink or swim with little money in a country where none of them belonged.

Barker had been a godsend. On his first day at Hat Creek he had met Barker, a strapping big man in a buffalo coat that made him seem even bigger. He had an easygoing, friendly way about him that made a man overlook the sharpness of his eyes. Barker heard Healy inquiring the route to Alder Gulch and Virginia City, in Montana.

"Been over that trail," he'd said. "Nothing easy about it."

"Could we make it? With the vans?"

Barker had glanced through the window at the vans. "Take money. You'd have to take off the wheels and put 'em on sled runners. And you'd have to have drivers who know this country in the winter."

Healy ordered drinks. "We've got to make the trip," he said, "and we can pay."

Barker glanced at the sign on the vans and his voice changed subtly. "Oh? You're Tom Healy? Of the Healy Shows?"

Healy had paid for the drinks with a gold piece.

"If you're serious," Barker told him, "I can furnish the drivers."

Nobody else offered any comment. One rough-hewn old man got abruptly to his feet and, after a quick, hard stare at Barker, walked out.

Barker knew the country and Barker could get the men. Out of insecurity and doubt came resolution, and the plans went forward. Barker would handle everything. "Just leave it to me," he told them.

Two drivers appeared. "Reliable," Barker said. "They worked for me before."

Wycoff was a stolid Pole with a heavy-featured, stupid-looking face. He had big, coarse hands and a hard jaw. He was heavy-shouldered and powerful. Art Boyle was a slender man with quick, prying eyes that seemed always to hold some secret, cynical amusement of their own.

Neither man impressed Healy, but Barker assured him he need not worry. Getting teamsters for a northern trip in winter was difficult, and these were good men.

Healy hesitated to ask questions, fearing to show his own ignorance, and equally afraid he would hear something that would make it impossible for him to delude himself any longer. Alder Gulch was the only way out.

And why should Barker say it could be done if it was impossible? He knew the country and was willing to go. Nonetheless, a rankling doubt remained. He stared gloomily at the snow-covered window and listened to the rising wind.

In the outer room there was boisterous laughter. He

listened, feeling doubt uneasy within him. Only the quiet courage of the girl at his side gave him strength. For the first time he began to appreciate his helplessness here, so far from the familiar lights and sounds of cities. He had never seen a map of Wyoming. He had only the vaguest idea of the location of Alder Gulch. He was a fool—a simple-minded, utterly ridiculous . . .

"I wish he was going with us."

He knew to whom she referred, and the same thought had occurred to him. "Barker doesn't like him."

"I know. He's a killer. Maybe an outlaw."

Wind whined under the eaves. Healy got to his feet and walked to the window. "He wouldn't come, anyway."

"No, I guess not. And trouble follows men like that." Janice came to him. "Don't worry, Tom. We'll make it."

Williams appeared in the door, drying his hands on a bar towel. "Some of the boys . . ." he began. Then he stopped. "Well, we were wondering if you folks would put on a show. We're all snowed in, like. The boys would pay. Take up a collection."

Healy hesitated. Why not? They could not leave before morning, anyway.

"We'd pay," Williams insisted. "They suggested it."

"You'll have to clear one end of the room," Healy said.

He started for the door, glancing back at Janice. She was looking out the window, and looking past her, he could see a man crunching over the snow toward the barn. It was King Mabry.

Tom Healy looked at Janice's expression and then at Mabry. He had reached the barn and was opening the door, a big, powerful man who knew this country and who walked strongly down a way he chose. Healy felt a pang of jealousy.

He pulled up short, considering that. *Him?* Jealous?

With a curiously empty feeling in his stomach he stared at the glowing stove in the next room. He was in love.

He was in love with Janice Ryan.

# Chapter Four

HE STOOD ALONE on the outer edge of the crowd that watched the show, a tall, straight man with just a little slope to his shoulders from riding the long trails.

He wore no gun in sight, but his thumbs were hooked in his belt and Janice had the feeling that the butt of a gun was just behind his hand. It would always be there.

The light from the coal-oil lamp on the wall touched his face, turning his cheeks into hollows of darkness and his eyes into shadows. He still wore his hat, shoved back from his face. He looked what he was, hard, tough . . . and lonely.

The thought came unbidden. He would always know loneliness. The mark of it was on him.

He was a man of violence. No sort of man she would ever have met at home . . . and no sort of man for her to know. Yet from her childhood she had heard of such men.

Watching from behind the edge of the blanket curtain, Janice remembered stories heard when she was a little girl, stories told by half-admiring men of duels and gun battles; but they had never known such a man as this, who walked in a lost world of his own creation.

Yet King Mabry was not unlike her father. Stern like him, yet with quiet humor sleeping at the corners of his eyes.

Maggie was out front now, holding them as she always held them with her tear-jerking monologues and her songs of lonely men. Her face was puffy under her too blonde hair, her voice hoarse from whisky and too many years on the boards, but she had them as not even Doc Guilford could get them. Because at heart all these men were sentimental.

All?

She looked again at King Mabry. Could a man be sentimental and kill eleven men?

And what sort of man was he?

The thought made her look for Benton, but he was nowhere in sight. Joe Noss stood near the door talking to Art Boyle. She thought the name, and then it registered in her consciousness and she looked again.

Yes, it was Barker's teamster. He stood very close to Noss, his eyes on the stage. But she knew he was listening to Noss.

The sight made her vaguely uneasy, yet there was nothing unusual in two men talking together in these cramped quarters, where sooner or later everybody must rub elbows with everybody else.

If Mabry was aware of their presence, he gave no indication. His concern seemed only with the show.

Dodie Saxon came up behind her and Janice drew aside so the younger girl could stand in the opening.

"Which one is King Mabry?" Dodie whispered.

Janice indicated the man standing quietly against the wall.

"He's handsome."

"He's a killer."

Janice spoke more sharply than she had intended. Dodie was too much interested in men, and this man was the wrong one in whom to be interested.

Dodie shrugged a shapely shoulder. "So? This is Wyoming, not Boston. It's different here."

"It's still killing." Janice turned sharply away. "You're on next, Dodie."

Dodie opened her coat, revealing her can-can costume. "I'm ready."

Mabry straightened from the wall as applause followed the end of Maggie's act. He turned his back on the stage and started toward the door.

"He's leaving," Janice said. Just why, she could not have explained, but she was secretly pleased.

Dodie threw off her coat and signaled Doc Guilford at

the piano for her cue. "He won't leave," she said pertly. "Not if he's the man I think he is!"

She moved into the steps of the can-can, and she moved to something more than music. Janice felt her cheeks flush self-consciously. Dodie had an exciting body that she knew very well how to use, and she delighted in the admiration of men. Yet tonight she was dancing for just one man, and Janice realized it with a pang of jealousy. Angrily she turned away, but her anger was for herself. It was silly to feel as she did when she was not interested in King Mabry, or likely to be.

Yet she turned and glanced back. Mabry had stopped at the sound of the music. Joe Noss had vanished, but Art Boyle remained where he had been, the stage receiving all his attention now.

As Dodie began to sing, her tall, graceful body moving with the music, Mabry dropped his hand from the door latch and walked back to the bar. The song was in French. Not more than one or two understood the words, but of the meaning there could be no doubt. It was pert and it was saucy. Mabry watched Dodie finish her act with a last flippant twist of her hips, and then Janice went on.

She sang the old songs, the heart songs, the songs of home sung to men who had no homes. She sang of love to men who knew only the casual women of frontier towns; of lilacs in bloom, of gaslight, of walking down shady lanes, all to men who knew only the raw backs of mountains, wilderness untamed and brutal.

She sang of peace to men who walked the hairline between life and the trigger finger. And she won them there as she never could have won them back East, where all that she sang of was available and present.

Tom Healy came to the bar and watched her, knowing with a sort of desperation that for him there could be no other girl; yet he knew she had never thought of him as husband or lover.

She was all he had ever wanted, all he could ever want.

"Ever been married, King?" he asked.

"Is it likely?"

"Neither have I."

Barker came into the room and paused, rolling a cigar between his lips as he watched Janice. From the corner of his mouth he spoke to Art Boyle, and Boyle turned instantly and left the room.

Barker crossed to the bar. Ignoring Mabry, he spoke to Healy. "The weather's broken. If you're ready, we can move out the first of the week."

"We'll be ready."

Healy had no enthusiasm in him. This was what he had wanted, but watching the girl who sang, he was uneasy. He had no right to take her off into the winter, to risk her life, or the lives of the others.

"Boyle's at work with another man. They'll get runners on the wagons. Then we can move."

Healy glanced at Mabry, but the gun fighter's face told him nothing.

"We'll need supplies," Barker added.

Healy drew his sack purse from his pocket and shook out three gold coins. Barker accepted them, his eyes estimating the sack.

Mabry turned abruptly and went outside. His shadow merged into the blackness near the station and he looked at the sky. Tomorrow he must go on to Cheyenne. It was as well. This was not his business.

The clouds had broken. It was warmer, and the wind had gone down. Behind the barn he could see the glow of lanterns. He crossed to the barn, the snow crunching under his heels.

Inside, the barn was lighted by the glow of two lanterns hanging from a two-by-four that ran down the center. He walked back to his horse, put more feed in the box, and checked the position of his saddle. For a long time he stood there, his hand on the cold leather.

It was not his business. Healy should know what he was doing. And he could be wrong about Barker.

Nevertheless, it was a fool play, starting into that country in the dead of winter with three women and wagons that heavy. And no roads . . . only horse trails at best. There was no way they could make it in less than a month, and it might take twice that.

Yet he remembered the light on Janice's face, and remembered her voice, reaching back into his boyhood with her songs. He swore softly. He should saddle up and get out. It was no place for him. No business of his. Healy was a good sort, but he was a fool.

Outside he could hear the voices and the hammering as the workmen removed wheels and put on runners.

The hostler came from his quarters in the corner of the barn.

"Them actors ain't showin' much sense."

Mabry made no comment.

"Rough country. No proper trails. An' they'll be buckin' the north wind most of the way."

"Know this man Barker?"

The hostler's talkative mood seemed to dissipate. He cleared his throat. "Gettin' late." He turned away, too quickly. "I better get some sleep."

Outside Mabry struck a match and looked at the thermometer. It was only two degrees below zero. Much better than the forty below it had been. By day, with the sun out, it would be good traveling.

No reason for him to interfere, and he had no time even if he wanted to. He was due in Cheyenne within forty-eight hours and he was not going to make it unless he rode the clock around. He had no business getting involved in whatever Barker was up to. Yet the thought rankled. . . .

Day broke cold and clear, but infinitely warmer than it had been for the past week. Mabry rolled out of bed with the first light and dressed swiftly. Nobody was awakened by his movements, and, gathering his gear, he stepped out into the passage.

Across the hall there were soft movements. He went into the empty saloon and, still carrying his gear, on to the dining room.

Williams was there, huddled over a pot of coffee, and Mabry picked up a cup and joined him.

The cook brought in their breakfast and Williams handed the coffeepot to Mabry. "You got to watch that Benton," Williams volunteered. "Griffin, too. They won't forget."

"Neither will I."

Janice came into the room suddenly, glancing at the two men. She sat down a little to one side, accepting her breakfast from the cook.

"You're leaving?"

At her question, Mabry nodded. Deliberately he tried to avoid conversation, but Janice persisted.

"You don't approve of our trip, do you?"

"No." He put down his cup. "None of my business."

"Why don't you approve?"

He said nothing, but continued to eat. Janice waited several minutes, then said, "I asked you why."

"No trip for women. Be bitter cold."

"And you don't like Andy Barker."

"That's right. I don't like him."

"Why?"

"No man goes off on a trip like that in winter unless something's wrong about it."

"You're traveling."

He smiled briefly, without humor. "And something's wrong. I've business in Cheyenne. After that, I'm on my own."

She considered that, then said, "I'll trust Tom Healy. He knows what he's doing."

"Maybe." He got up, not wanting to continue. "And maybe he doesn't know what he's doing."

"Talking about me?"

Tom Healy stood in the doorway. There was no humor in him now. He walked on into the room and faced

Mabry across the table. When he spoke his voice was low but positive.

"This company is my business. We won't do any business between Cheyenne and Salt Lake with bigger companies ahead of us. We're going to Alder Gulch. You don't think I know what I'm doing. I do."

"None of my business. You handle it your way."

He gathered his gear and went out the door with Healy looking after him. More than anything else, Healy wanted Mabry with them, respecting the knowledge the other man possessed, knowledge and experience he dearly needed. Yet it was not in him to ask. Had Janice not been there, he might have suggested it, but having seen the way she looked at Mabry, Healy knew he did not want Mabry along.

At the door, Mabry turned. He looked past Healy at Janice and said, "Luck."

His shoulders filled the doorway as he went out. For several minutes after he was gone nobody said anything.

"Knew him in Dodge," Williams said suddenly, "and again in Utah. He's salty."

"Has he really killed so many men?"

"He has. Killed one at Doan's store. Fellow name of Les Benham was going to cut Mabry's herd. Mabry said he wasn't."

"Did they cut it?"

"Too busy burying Les Benham."

Across the road in a small cabin Griffin looked up from his bunk. His shoulder was on the mend, but he was feeling weak.

Barker nodded toward the curtained doorway. "Anybody in there?"

"We're alone. What's on your mind?"

"Two hundred fast dollars for you."

"Never started a conversation better." Griffin sat up and began to roll a smoke. "What's the story?"

"Two hundred dollars if Mabry doesn't last out the week."

"No."

"No?"

"I want to spend the money I make."

"Scared?" Barker sneered.

"You bet I am. I don't want any part of him."

"Three hundred?"

Griffin said nothing and Barker waited. He did not want to go higher, but remembering Janice, he knew that more than money was involved. He had rarely wanted one woman more than another, but he wanted this one.

Moreover, there was three hundred in that small sack of Healy's, and if the information from his spy in the bank was correct, there was fifteen thousand in gold hidden in those show wagons.

Mabry might ride away, but Barker was no gambler. And he had seen the way Mabry and Janice looked at each other. There was no place in his plans for interference by a man of Mabry's caliber.

"No," Griffin said at last, "I won't touch it."

"I'd think you'd hate his guts."

"Mabry?" Griffin's eyes were venomous. "I do. I'd kill him in a minute if it was safe."

"There's no reason he should even see you."

Griffin stared at the comforter on the bed. He hated snow and cold, and with money in his pocket he could go to California. California would be nice this time of year. He'd worked for Hunter quite a spell, or he would never have gone after Mabry for him, but knowing Hunter, he did not want to return and report his failure. The old man had a reputation as an honest cattleman and he did not like hired gunmen who were able to talk. But California was no good to a dead man.

"They wouldn't find him until spring," Barker argued, "if they ever found him. You could be a hundred yards off, and if you missed you'd have time for another shot."

Mabry had only two hands. He was only a man, and Griffin had never been bested with a rifle. Bellied down in the snow with a good field of fire . . .

Griffin threw his cigarette into the fire. "I'd want it in gold."

"Half tonight, the rest when the job is done."

Barker must feel those wagons carried real money. Maybe he could get in on . . . No, not where women were involved. You could steal horses and kill sheep, you could even murder a man in broad daylight and have a chance, but if you molested a decent woman you were in real trouble.

He shoved a chunk of wood into the potbellied stove. What kind of a man had he become? Once he would have shot a man for even suggesting that he hire his gun. Now was he ready to take money for murder? With Hunter, the brand had been involved, a ranch he was riding for. But this was murder.

Where was it a man made the turn? What happened to change him? He had once been a kid with ideals. . . .

"All right," he said, "get me the money."

That was the kind of man he had become.

# Chapter Five

KING MABRY had been absent five days when he crossed the creek again and rode up to Hat Creek Stage Station. He told himself he was a fool to return here and to half kill a horse and himself to do it. Yet the thought of Healy's taking off into the winter with those women angered him.

The least he could do was ride along and see that they made it. After all, he was going in that general direction himself.

Yet when the station came in sight there were no vans and no evidence of activity.

Suddenly worried, he came down the hill at a spanking trot. At the barn he swung around behind it. The vans were gone!

The hostler came to the door as he swung down. "That black of yours is gettin' mighty restless. He'll be glad to see you."

"When did they pull out?"

"The show folks?" The hostler stoked his pipe. "Day after you did. Barker, he was in a fret to get off. They figured on leavin' today, but he'd have it no way but to start right off. Said the weather was just right."

Mabry looked at the snow-covered fields. He could see the ruts in the snow left by sled runners.

"Switch saddles," he said. "I'll be riding."

The hostler hesitated. "That there Griffin," he said, looking carefully around, "he's been askin' after you. Ever' day he comes to see is your horse still here."

Crossing to the stage station, Mabry ate hurriedly and got what supplies he would need. As he went through the saloon he saw Griffin sitting at a table idly riffling cards.

Following the southern slope of the hills, Mabry rode westward. The air was crisp and cold. There was no wind and the smoke of the chimneys at Hat Creek had lifted straight into the sky. The black horse was impatient, tugging at the bit. "Going home, boy?" Mabry asked him. "Back to Wind River?"

Rising over the crest of a hill, the black's ears went up suddenly and Mabry turned in the saddle to look where the horse was looking.

Nothing. . . .

He was not fooled. The black horse was mountain bred, born to wild country. He had seen or smelled something.

Mabry swung down the slope to the edge of the trees and skirted the timber, keeping the line of trees between himself and the direction of the horse's attention.

This was an old game, one he had played too often to be easily trapped. Whoever was out there must be trailing the vans or himself. He changed direction several times, avoiding snow fields and keeping to hard ground.

Barker had camped at Lance Creek the first night out. Seeing that, Mabry pushed on. The black horse ate up space and that night they camped at a spot Mabry chose as he rode past. Riding by, he swung wide and circled back, camping where he could watch his own trail.

He made shelter for himself and his horse in a matter of minutes. He cut partly through a small tree, then broke it over to the ground, trimming out the branches on the under side, leaving those on top and at the sides. The cut branches he piled on top or wove into the sides. With other boughs he made a bed inside on the snow.

He tied his horse under a thick-needled evergreen close by, then wove branches into the brush for a windbreak.

Over a small fire he made coffee and a thick stew. When he had eaten he rolled in his blankets and closed his eyes for sleep.

Before he slept he thought of Janice. Yet it was foolish to think. What could there be with him for any girl? He was a warrior in a land growing tame.

The wind rose and moaned low in the evergreens. The coals of the fire glowed deeply red against the dark. Irritably he thought of Healy and the company up ahead. They were making good time, getting farther and farther from any possible help or interference, farther into this wide, white land of snow and loneliness. Barker had rushed them out of Hat Creek . . . to get them away before Mabry returned?

Most men would not have taken that ride to Cheyenne, but he had accepted the job offered in good faith, and only after he arrived in Deadwood did he discover that he had been hired for his gun rather than for his knowledge of cattle.

He had been hired to ramrod a tough cow outfit, which was all right, but it meant pushing the Sioux off their hunting grounds and killing any that objected. He had been hired because of his reputation, and he wanted no part of it.

He said as much in Cheyenne. That was what he told Old Man Hunter when he told him what he could do with his job. And what he would do if Hunter sent any more killers after him.

A cold branch rattled its frozen fingers. Snow whispered against the boughs of his shelter. He slept.

During the brief halt when they stopped the teams for a breather at the top of a long hill, Tom Healy ran ahead and rapped on the door of the women's wagon.

Dodie opened the door and he scrambled in. His face was red with cold, but he was smiling.

Inside the wagon the air was warm and close. Along one side were two bunks, narrow but sufficient. On the other side was one bunk and a table that was no more than a shelf. On it was a washbasin and a small cask filled with water. In the front of the wagon was a potbellied stove.

Under the bunks were chests for the packing of clothing. At the end of each bunk was a small closet for hanging clothes. It was neat, compact, and well ordered.

The van in which the two men rode was built along the same lines, but with just two bunks and more storage space. In each van there were two lanterns, an ax, and a shovel. In each van there was stored a considerable supply of food, with the larger amount in the van where the men lived. On top of each van was a canvas-covered roll of old backdrops and scenes used in some of the various melodramas that were the troupe's stock in trade.

"Frosty out there," Healy said.

"We're making good time, aren't we?" Janice asked.

"Better than on wheels. The snow's frozen over and we're moving right along."

He did not add what was on his mind, that they had better make good time. As long as the surface was hard, they could keep going, and so far the horses had found grass enough, but the distance was beginning to seem interminable. For the first time Healy was realizing what distance meant in the West.

Four days now and they had seen nobody, and nothing but snow-covered hills and streams lined with trees and brush. And there were long levels where snow drifted endlessly like sand on the desert. And always the cold.

Four days, and they had only begun. Yet they had made good time and that worried him. It seemed that Barker was pushing faster than necessary. Yet he hesitated to interfere. Perhaps Barker only wanted to get them out of this open country before another blizzard struck.

Janice slipped into her coat, throwing her hair over the collar. "Tom, I want to walk a little. Do you want to join me?"

They sprang down, hand in hand, and stepped off to the side, starting on ahead.

Barker was sitting his horse, lighting a cigar as they drew abreast of him. He gave them a brief smile. "Cold for walking. Never liked it, myself."

"Do us good," Janice said, and they walked on.

All around was an immensity of snow-covered plains

and low hills, here and there cut by the dark line of a
ravine. There were many streams, their names singing a
sort of wild saga, filled with poetry. Lance Creek, Little
Lightning, Old Woman Creek farther back, and Twenty
Mile close by.

"Worried, Tom?"

The question startled him. "Is it that obvious?"

"I thought you were." They walked three or four
steps. "Why?"

He groped for easy words. "The distance, I guess. It's
this country. It's too big."

"How far do we have to go?"

Healy side-stepped that question. He did not even like
to think of it himself. They walked on, plowed through
some snow, and stopped on a ridge. The wind had an
edge when it touched the skin. He warmed his face
against his hands.

"Tom!" Janice was pointing, and his eyes followed
her finger to a row of tracks in the snow. Walking on,
they came to the tracks and stopped. They were the
tracks of a single horse, cutting across the route of the
wagons and disappearing over the hills.

At their wild gesturing, Barker put his horse to a gallop
and rode up to them.

"Indians!" Healy said, indicating the tracks.

Astride his horse, Barker seemed unusually big, indomitable. Yet his face grew cold as he looked at the line
of tracks. They were those of a shod horse, going off
across the country in a direction where nothing lay.

No white man in his right mind would be riding away
from any known shelter in the dead of winter.

"Shod horse," he said briefly. "It wasn't an Indian."

That Barker was disturbed was obvious. Healy watched
him, curious as to why the tracks of a white man should
upset him so.

Barker turned sharply to Janice. "Did that Mabry fellow say anything about catching up?"

"No. Why should he?"

Yet, remembering the way he had looked at her, Janice wondered, too, and blushed at the memory. But she should not think of such a man. He was a killer, probably completely vicious under that quiet exterior.

The mark of the country was on him. Seeing it now, getting the feel of it for the first time, Janice could understand it. He carried the mark of a wild land, a land that was itself aloof and poised. A land where you lost yourself, as they did now, in immeasurable distance.

Day after day the wagons had plodded on, and day after day the snow-covered hills fell behind, the streams were crossed, the lonely camps abandoned to the wilderness. And day after day she seemed to dwindle, to grow less. The vans were tiny things, their bright-colored sides tawdry in the stillness and snow. All was immensity where they seemed to crawl at a snail's pace into a vastness beyond belief.

They were alien here . . . or was it only she? With a kind of resentment, she saw how easily Dodie fitted into the landscape, how easily she did the little things around the campfire. Even Healy had seemed to grow, to expand. He seemed bigger, somehow, more of a man. Yet the distance and the cold depressed her, the flat and endless sky made her eager to be back inside.

The vans were coming along now. Barker had walked his horse back to them. Had his manner changed? Or was she imagining things? He was impatient with their questions, even irritable.

Steam rose from the flanks of the horses, and from their nostrils. Travel was easier because the hard snow crusted the ground, covering the unevenness and the stones. The hills drew closer, lifting their snow-clad summits higher against the dull gray sky. The southern extremity, Barker had said, of the Big Horns.

After the fresh, clear air, the hot confines of the van seemed unbelievably close. Yet she was glad to be inside. Maggie was knitting. Dodie lay on her back, reading a copy of *Harper's Weekly*.

"Nice walk?" Dodie looked past her magazine at them.

"Wonderful! You should try it!"

"She won't," Maggie said cuttingly. "Not unless she can see some men."

"I don't want to see men." Dodie preened herself ostentatiously. "I want them to see me."

"With that walk," Maggie said sarcastically, "they'll see you!"

"You're just jealous."

"Jealous?" Maggie flounced. "When I was your age I not only got the men—I knew what to do with them!"

Dodie arched her back luxuriously, like a sleek kitten. "I'll learn," she said complacently. "Somebody will teach me."

Tom Healy was amused. "Careful. You'll get the last lesson first."

Dodie looked at him, wide-eyed with innocence. "But I *always* read the end of a book first!"

## Chapter Six

THE WEATHER HELD and the trail was good. They made twenty miles that day and as much the day following. The mountains loomed over them, snow-covered and aloof.

There was no rest. Each morning they started early, and the noon halts were short. Healy watched the trail and saw that Barker selected it with care. The way might be the longest around, but invariably it was the best for traveling, and they made time.

The cold held, though the skies were usually clear. Sometimes he walked far ahead with Janice, watching the wagons come along after them, but it was only among hills that they could do this, for on comparatively level country the wagons moved at a good clip.

From the distance the two garishly painted wagons with their teams seemed grotesquely out of place in this vast wilderness.

Barker was restless and increasingly brusque. Only the fact that they were miles from anywhere and completely in Barker's hands kept Healy from a showdown with him. Several times during halts he found Barker in low-voiced conversation with Wycoff and Boyle, conversations that ceased abruptly when Healy appeared.

More and more Barker's unwillingness to have Mabry along occupied Healy's thoughts. In a country where every pair of hands was a help, Barker had been unwilling to let anyone else accompany them.

Once, stuck in deep snow in a bottom, they were hours getting out, and made it only with everyone, the girls included, pushing. Twice they had to hitch both teams to a wagon to draw them up steep hills.

He found himself watching the backtrail, almost hoping Mabry would appear. Yet there was no reason he should join them, and no reason they should expect him. The identity of the rider of the shod horse puzzled him. He gathered from comments he heard and from campfire talk that there was nothing off to the north for more than a hundred miles. Yet that was the direction the rider had taken.

Once, off to one side, he found the remains of a small fire and boot tracks around it. He did not mention his discovery when he returned. Another time he found where someone had watched them from a distance, but the man wore square-toed boots, not at all like Mabry's.

Returning to the wagon, he found Doc Guilford on the edge of his bunk playing solitaire. "How's it look?"

Healy glanced at him. Doc was a wise old man. "Not good. Something about Barker I don't like."

"Reminds me of a con man I knew once," Guilford mused, "only this one is tougher and meaner."

Healy watched Doc's game. He was himself changing, and the country was doing it. He was wary in a way he had never been before.

"Got a gun?"

Doc did not seem surprised. "Uh-huh."

"Keep it handy."

"I do." Doc placed a red card carefully. "Lately."

The mountains loomed nearer now. A long red wall of sandstorm shut them off from the west, disappearing to the north, farther than they could see.

The going was slower as they crossed more and more streams. They followed no trail, for there was none. Perhaps a horse trail, but even this they could not see under the snow.

Barker explained during a halt. "Passes north are all closed by now. We'll use the Hole-in-the-Wall. Only opening in nearly forty miles. Place where the Cheyennes under Dull Knife came after the Custer fight."

"We can get through?"

"Uh-huh. Little stream flows through. A fork of the Powder. Wild country beyond, but I know my way through."

There were no more tracks, yet Barker kept looking for them and he was uneasy. When they camped again it was in a bend of the stream in the wide gap of the red wall. All around them was hard-packed snow.

The wagons formed a V against the wind. Boyle put sticks together and made a fire while Wycoff led the horses to the stream, breaking the ice so they could drink.

Healy gathered fuel, ranging along the stream's bank for driftwood. Janice came out of the wagon and joined him, her cheeks flushed with cold, eyes sparkling.

"Like it?" he asked appreciatively.

"Love it!"

She gathered sticks and threw them into a pile. Seeing a large deadfall, a cottonwood blown down in some storm and floated here by some flood, she pushed through the brush to get the bark. Then she stood very still.

After a moment she walked ahead, then paused again. She turned and called softly, "Tom!"

He came quickly, clutching a heavy stick. When he saw her alone and unharmed he lowered the stick and walked up. "What's the matter?"

"I heard something. Someone was moving in the brush over there."

Behind them there was a sudden crunching of footsteps.

Art Boyle pushed through the brush and stopped. There was a knowing leer in his eyes. "Sorry." He grinned. "Huntin' wood?"

"I piled some back there." Janice pointed.

When he had gone, she turned to Healy. "Tom, what does it mean?"

"I don't know," he admitted reluctantly, "only the more I think about it, the less I like it. They never want

any of us out of their sight, and for some reason Barker
doesn't want to see anybody and doesn't want anybody
to see us."

"Why?"

"I wish I knew."

"Tom, do you suppose . . . I mean, could they be
planning to rob us?"

He considered that. Certainly they gave no evidence of
being supplied with more than barely sufficient funds.
The outfit would be worth something . . . and they
could not know about the money concealed in the wagon.
Or could they?

And if they were robbed and murdered, who would
know?

In more than a week they had seen nobody, and only
the tracks of two riders, neither of whom would ap-
proach them.

Tom Healy looked at the wide gate of the Hole-in-the-
Wall. Far behind them were Cheyenne and Deadwood.
To the west, through that gate, lay endless miles of
wilderness before they would come to Salt Lake.

Western Wyoming was almost empty of white men, a
wild and broken land where their two wagons would be
lost in a vast white world of snow, mountains, and rivers.
Nobody expected them in Alder Gulch. There was Maguire in Butte, but he was expecting to hear from them
in Salt Lake, where the money was to be deposited for
him. If anything happened out here it would be months
before they were missed.

Healy's face was drawn with worry. "Maybe we're
imagining things," he said. "Nothing's gone wrong yet."

"Tom, who could have made those tracks?"

"No idea."

"King Mabry?"

"Could be." He looked at her thoughtfully. "Like
him?"

"I don't know. I don't know at all. I feel I shouldn't
like him, yet . . . well, there's something about him."

"I know." He sighed. "Well, we'd best get back. It's almost dark."

As they walked they picked up what dry wood they saw.

"I don't like him," Healy admitted, "because he likes you."

She laughed. "Why, Tom!"

"All right, so I'm stupid."

"Anyway, I'm sure he doesn't like me. He thinks I'm a nuisance."

"Maybe." Healy looked at the wall of sandstone, etched hard against the gray sky of coming night. "Like him or not, I'd give the proceeds of our next ten weeks to know he was close by. This place is beyond me, much as I hate to admit it. I'm out of my depth."

She said nothing, for there was nothing to say. Tom Healy, a quiet Irish singer, accustomed until now to the life of the Eastern theatres and cities, was out of his depth. Yet other than Tom there was only an old man who bragged of bygone days and played solitaire.

Barker was a big man, a powerful man. Then there were the sly, sneering Art Boyle and the dull, animal-like Wycoff. It was not pretty to think of.

But was today a deadline? Because tomorrow they would be beyond the Wall? Because it was a dividing line?

They dumped their wood beside the fire. Boyle had water on and was cooking. The fire was sheltered and the food smelled good.

Wycoff came into the circle of light wiping his hands on his buckskins. He looked across the fire at Dodie, his deep-set eyes invisible in the shadows under his brows.

Barker seemed restless, and only after a long time would he sit down.

There was a subtle change in the atmosphere, something in the manner of Wycoff and Boyle that had not been present before. When Wycoff shouldered past Maggie, he almost pushed her. Healy started to protest, then held his peace.

Doc Guilford sat back from the fire with his shoulders against a wheel. His shrewd eyes were curiously alive, and they rarely left Barker.

There was no talk during supper and Maggie was the first to go to the wagon. She was not well, she said. Yet nobody paid much attention.

Dodie got up to leave, and Boyle, who was relaxed on one elbow, looked around. "Stick around, honey. Night's young."

She merely looked at him and walked on to the wagon. He sat up, staring after her, his face sullen.

Janice got up and scoured her cup with snow. Guilford had not moved. He sat by the wagon wheel, warming his hands inside his coat.

Healy's scalp began to tighten. Maybe it was Boyle's surly attitude, or something in Wycoff's careless brutality. Suddenly Healy knew the warning had come too late. The time was now.

Tom Healy got up and stretched. There was a shotgun in the wagon. It was hidden beneath his blankets. There were shells there, too, but the shotgun was already loaded. He had to have that shotgun and have it now. He started for the wagon.

Behind him Boyle spoke impatiently. "What are we waiting for, Barker? Damn it, I'm—"

"Healy!" Barker's voice caught him full in the light and two good steps from the wagon.

Healy turned. "Yeah? I'm tired. Figured I'd catch some sleep."

Guilford had not moved. He sat very quietly against the wheel, but he was alert.

Barker's gun appeared from beneath his coat. "Come back and sit down, Healy. We want to talk."

"I'm all right where I am. Start talking."

Barker balanced the gun against the butt of his palm. "Where's the money, Healy? Where's that strongbox?"

Tom Healy took his time, trying to think of a way out. He desperately needed a hole card and he had none. Barker would not hesitate to kill, and he would be of no use to the girls dead.

"You boys have it wrong. There isn't enough money in that box to keep you drunk a week."

"He's lyin'!" Boyle shouted. "Damn it, Barker, you said he must be carrying four, five thousand, anyway."

"There's not eight hundred dollars among the lot of us," Healy said. "That's why we're so anxious to reach the Gulch." He took a careful breath. "No use you boys going off half-cocked. I know this is a rough trip. I'll give you seven hundred more to take us on through."

Barker smiled, showing his white teeth under his mustache. "And what would you tell them at the Gulch? What nice boys we'd been? I don't think so, Healy. I think this is as far as we go."

"Anyway," Boyle said, "it's as far as you go."

Wycoff looked up from under thick brows, grinning at Healy. Barker's gun tilted and Healy saw his finger tense. He threw himself desperately at a hole in the wall of brush.

Barker's gun blasted once, then again. He hit the brush, tripped, and plunged face down and sliding in the snow. A bullet whipped past him and then he was up and running. Inside him was a desperate hope that unless they could be sure of killing them all, they would not dare kill any. If he got safely away, they might hesitate to kill the women while he might remain to tell the story.

He stopped suddenly, knowing the noise he made, and moved behind a blacker bush. There was no pursuit. From where he now stood, on a slight rise, he could see part of the camp.

He was fifty yards off, but in the clear, cold air the voices were as plain as if he stood among them.

"Shot me," Wycoff said. "The old devil shot me."

Guilford no longer sat straight against the wheel. He was slumped over on his side, limp and still.

"It was me he shot at," Barker said. "You just got in the way."

"Well," Wycoff shouted, "don't stand there! Get me a bandage! I'm bleedin'!"

"Aw, quit cryin'!" Boyle was impatient. "He just nicked you, an' it's over. We got 'em."

Tom Healy looked around for a way to run. He might have to go fast, for without doubt they would come looking for him.

Only they did not have to look now. They could wait until morning, then mount their horses and ride him down in the snow. He was unarmed and helpless.

Inside the wagon, three women stared at each other, listening. Janice got up and started for the door, but Maggie caught her arm. "Don't go out! The door's locked now and it won't be easy to break."

"There's a shotgun in the other wagon," Janice said.

Dodie swung her legs to the floor and began dressing. Then she opened her small carpetbag. When she straightened up she held a long Colt pistol in her hand.

Janice stared. "Where did you get that?"

"It belonged to my father. Can you shoot it?"

"Yes," Janice said.

She took the pistol. It was very heavy and it was loaded. She carried it to her bunk and put it down. It they tried to break in, that would be the time to use it.

"Tom got away," Maggie whispered.

"Yes, but it's awfully cold away from the fire."

Wind rattled along the side of the van, moving a lantern that hung outside. They heard a mutter of voices.

Silently they waited in the dark wagon, making no sound, huddled together with blankets around their shoulders. It was a long time until morning.

A hand tried the door, then pushed. After a moment footsteps retreated and there was a further mutter of talk.

The wind began to pick up. Blown snow, frozen long since, rattled along the side walls.

It was very cold. . . .

## Chapter Seven

OUT IN THE DARKNESS Tom Healy crouched and shuddered with cold. He had to have a fire. Much as he hated to move far from the wagons, he must have a fire.

There was nothing he could do here. And it was improbable that anything further would be done tonight. He had seen Boyle try the door of the women's van, swear, and turn away. The three men huddled close to the fire, talking in low tones.

Healy straightened stiffly and walked over the snow. A half mile away, among some rocks and trees, he found shelter from the wind. Shivering, he got sticks together and started a fire.

He had no gun. He had no weapon of any sort. The night wind blew cold, and his blaze dipped and fluttered, then ate hungrily at the dry sticks.

Doc Guilford was dead. The old man had made his try and failed. Wycoff's wound was too slight to matter.

In the morning they would rifle the wagons. They would find the money belonging to the show, but the other box might not be so easily found. It was sunk in a compartment of the double bottom of the wagon. Maguire himself had suggested the hiding place in his letter. They would also find the shotgun.

The shotgun. If he could get his hands on that shotgun. He considered the possibility as the fire slowly warmed his cold muscles. His chances were slight, yet if he got the shotgun he could handle that crowd. At close range it was hard to miss with a shotgun.

He had no experience on which to draw. His years began to seem woefully wasted, for in this emergency he had nothing on which to base his plans but remembered sequences of old melodramas or the stories of Ned Buntline. Yet if he could creep close enough, if he could get into that wagon . . .

First he must give them time to fall asleep. He fed fuel to his fire, reflecting that if the fire did not keep him warm, getting fuel for it would. Searching for wood, he found a hefty club. With that he felt better.

An hour passed slowly and he waited it out. His back was cold, his face too hot, yet he felt better. He was no longer shaking, and he had a plan.

When the third hour had passed he left his fire burning and, taking the club, started back to the wagons.

Art Boyle dozed on a blanket near the fire. The others had gone to sleep, as they usually did, in hastily built shelters near the wagons. Healy waited, hoping Boyle would fall asleep, yet after several minutes he knew that he must act at once, before he grew too cold.

The door of the van where he had himself slept was close by. Neither Wycoff nor Barker had moved in.

The hinges were well oiled and they should not squeak. There might be some frozen snow around the bottom of the door.

Mentally he went through every move. It would take four strides to cover the ground to the door. All would be within plain view of the man by the fire.

Once there, he must open the door without noise, step completely inside, and reach under the blanket where the shotgun lay. He must grasp it and turn, one hand on the barrel, the other at the trigger guard.

Once that turn was completed, he would be reasonably secure. He would disarm Boyle and tie him up, and then he would take Wycoff and Barker. One wrong move and he must shoot.

If he failed, he would be killed, and worse, Janice would be left without protection.

Janice and Dodie and Maggie . . . and it was his fault. He had brought them into this.

His mouth was dry and his heart pounding. He took one quick glance toward the still figure by the fire and stepped out toward the wagon. To him every footstep sounded horribly loud, yet the man lay still.

One . . . two . . . three . . . He was at the step. His hand grasped the latch and pulled. The door did not budge.

The mud and snow on the bottom had frozen.

He took a breath, then pulled hard on the door. It came open suddenly and he went through the door in one quick step. Outside there was no sound, and he moved swiftly to the bed, feeling for the shotgun.

"All right, Healy. Lift your hands—an' they better be empty!"

For an instant he wanted to gamble. He wanted to grasp the gun, swing it clear of the bedding. But he knew he would never make it.

He turned slowly. "Boyle." He took a breath, one hand still on the bed. Under it he could feel the outline of the shotgun barrel. "Boyle, there's not much here. Suppose you take what there is, give me that gun, and you take a horse and ride. How about it?"

"Not a chance!" Boyle's black frame in the doorway receded a little. "Come out with your hands up."

To make a move now would be certain death, and a dead man was no good to anybody.

"You won't get away with this. King Mabry's out there."

Art Boyle's grin showed in the reflected firelight. "If he's alive, he's got his own troubles."

"What's that mean?"

"Get down on the ground," Boyle said, and when Healy had descended, Boyle pushed the door shut. "Means the boss sent a man out to get him."

Healy was an actor and he threw on his talent now. "You sent *one* man after him? Hardly seems enough."

"He'll take him." Boyle said it, but to Healy he did not sound positive.

"Look, Boyle." Healy's voice was low and persuasive. "Why run a chance? There's seven hundred dollars in that wagon. Take it, take a horse, and beat it. Just let me have my chance. Then you'll have the money, and if Mabry comes you'll be out of it."

Boyle chuckled. "Might take it," he said, "was there only you. But there's them women. They're the best-lookin' women hit this country since I been here. I ain't goin' to miss that."

Healy searched his mind for an argument. Somebody was stirring in the shelter where Barker slept. The low murmur of their voices might awaken Barker.

Art Boyle stood six feet away, and Healy gauged the distance and considered it. Yet the sound of a shot would be an end to it.

Janice awakened suddenly. For an instant she lay perfectly still. Then she heard the low sound of voices and she slipped from her narrow bunk and listened.

Tom was out there! He was talking to someone. She strove to hear, then to see out. Finally, standing on tiptoe to look over the frost on the window, she made out Tom. She could not see who talked to him. Yet from his attitude she knew he was again a prisoner. She turned quickly for the gun.

Maggie moved, putting her feet to the floor and dragging her heavy coat around her. She picked up a heavy flatiron and hefted it. Dodie was awake, lying there, eyes wide, watching.

Janice waited for the other man to speak so she could locate his position. She would have to open the door, then shoot. And she had no idea whether she could score a hit or not. Yet it might give Tom a chance to do something.

She dropped a hand to the door latch, testing it gently. As they had been coming and going earlier in the day, the door was not frozen. She swung it open a few inches and heard Tom say:

"Whoever's out after Mabry will get killed. Mabry will find he's being trailed, and when he's through with the trailer he'll come hunting Barker."

"Might, at that," Boyle agreed. He seemed to be weighing his chances. "But I'd as soon take a chance with him as with Barker. Mabry's one man, Barker's got friends. Some of the old Plummer outfit."

"Plummer?"

"Sheriff one time up at Alder. His outfit murdered more'n a hundred people. Then the vigilantes hung twenty-six of the gang. But they didn't get 'em all."

Janice had the door opened wider now and was edging around to try a shot when Barker spoke. "What's going on?" Then, seeing Healy, he grinned. "Got him, did you?"

He walked over to Healy, lifted a broad hand, and struck him across the face. "I think I'll kill you now, before we have more trouble."

"Boss?" Boyle said.

"Well, what is it?"

"If we have to move these wagons, we can use him. Might's well get some work out of him first."

Barker hesitated, then shrugged. "All right. But for now, tie his hands and keep him with you. I want to go through that wagon."

Janice eased the door shut. She turned back to her bed. Her spirits had never been lower, and Maggie felt the same, obviously. They had done nothing. There had been nothing to do.

"What'll we do?" Dodie whispered.

And the whisper was like a plaintive cry in the lost emptiness of night.

## Chapter Eight

KING MABRY reached the Hole-in-the-Wall hours before the wagons arrived and followed a stream that he took to be the Middle Fork of the Powder, hunting a place to hole up for the night.

When he had ridden more than a mile he turned off into a ravine and found a place where the clay shoulder broke the wind. There he dug a shelter out of a snowbank.

The night was cold, but he was asleep before he was fairly settled in place.

At daybreak he thrust an arm from under the robe long enough to toss a couple of sticks on the coals. When they blazed up, he added more. Not until the fire was blazing cheerfully did he come out from under and pull on his heavy socks and moccasins.

When the coffee water was on, he mounted the bank to look around. The snow was unbroken as far as he could see except by the towering wall of red sandstone, and that was streaked with white where snow lay along the ledges and breaks.

He ate jerked beef and drank coffee, then saddled up and cut across the flatland toward the gap.

Nothing had come through. Had they gone up the valley of the Powder?

The sky was gray and lowering. It looked and felt like snow. He turned back toward the Hole, keeping to low ground and riding with caution. Yet he was almost at the opening itself before he heard the sound of an ax.

It was unmistakable. He listened, trying to place the sound exactly while the big horse stamped restlessly, eager to be moving.

He started again, riding directly toward the Wall.

There was little cover, but the stream had cut deep here and there, and the banks provided some concealment. There were some willows and here and there a cottonwood.

After a few minutes he saw the smoke. The darker gray of the morning clouds had disguised it well. When he was approximately four hundred yards away he drew up and left his horse in a space between the willows and a clay bank.

The sound of the ax continued.

It was late. If they were cutting wood, it meant they did not plan to move that day. Yet Barker must know what the sky implied. He would know it meant snow, and farther west the timber was fairly heavy along the streams, offering plenty of fuel. Here there were only willows and what driftwood they could find along the stream.

Carrying his rifle, he went downstream, covering the ground in long, easy strides. Pausing once, he cleared the rifle's mechanism to be sure that dampness had not frozen it tight.

When he worked his way to the top of the bank again he could see the vans. The stove in one of the wagons was going, and there was a fire beyond it.

As he watched, Healy came out of the willow carrying an armful of wood. Wycoff, one arm in a sling and his rifle in the other hand, walked a little to his left. Healy dumped the wood and started back toward the willows.

Edging around for a better view, Mabry saw Barker. But Art Boyle was nowhere in sight.

The small camp was concealed partly by the V of the two vans, forming a wall against the wind. A clay bank was to the west, and a hedge of willows protected the other two sides. Barker was sitting on a log drinking coffee. None of the women was in sight, and there was no sign of Doc Guilford.

Obviously, Barker had made his move. Wycoff's injured arm could be a result. What Barker now intended was not apparent, except that he planned to spend the night, yet in this weather that could easily mean being snowed in for a week. And his present position was far from good. Why wasn't he moving?

It was growing colder. Tying his scarf across his mouth to conceal his breath, he worked his way nearer.

He could do nothing without knowing where Boyle was. To make a move without knowing the whereabouts of all three men would be reckless in the extreme, and a man did not live long by being reckless. Only fools took chances.

It began to snow. Large flakes began to sift down from the gray sky, fast and thick. His coat began to whiten. He wiped off the rifle.

Healy was swinging an ax awkwardly, chopping a log. Wycoff was standing nearby, carrying the rifle in the hollow of his good arm.

Neither man was talking and Healy was obviously all in. The unfamiliar work and the cold were exhausting him. Wycoff chewed tobacco and watched, his features expressionless.

Healy stopped suddenly. "Got to take a breather," Mabry heard him say. "I never used an ax before."

"I can see that." Wycoff was contemptuous.

"What's Barker figure to do?" Healy asked.

Wycoff shrugged, saying nothing. Obviously he believed it was no concern of Healy's.

"He might get away with killing us, but if he touches the girls, he's in trouble."

"Our business," Wycoff said. "You get busy."

Healy picked up the ax and started a swing. Mabry eased back carefully, making no sound. Not a word about either Doc Guilford or Boyle.

He began to scout the vicinity. He was no longer worried about tracks, for in this snow they would soon be gone. He had circled well to the east, between the wagons and the Hole, when suddenly he stopped.

The body of a man lay sprawled across the wash ahead of him. A man that was no longer alive.

Moving to the body, Mabry looked down into the features of Doc Guilford. The old actor stared up at the sky, his sightless eyes staring at the falling snow. A flake touched an eyeball and remained there. The creases in his clothes and the tired lines of his face had become a web of white lines from the snow.

If Barker had killed this man, he dared not let the others live. So why was he waiting? And why here, of all places?

Mabry thought of the man who had been following him. He had led the fellow into the broken country to the south and then switched back north, traveling on rock to leave few tracks. Eventually the tracker would work out his trail and come up with him, and he might have a rendezvous with Barker at this point.

Suddenly he heard voices. One of them he instantly recognized as Boyle's. The teamster was alive, then, and still present.

Mabry saw Healy come in with an armful of wood, and they let him rest. Wycoff swore as he bumped his arm.

"What the hell?" Boyle was impatient. "Why not bust the wagon open and take them out?"

"Let them starve for a while," Barker said. "They'll listen better if they do."

"To the devil with that!" Boyle kicked angrily at a stick. "We'd better burn those wagons and get out of here. I don't like the feel of this place."

Barker said nothing, but after thinking it over he got up and walked to the wagon door. "All right!" he spoke impatiently. "Open up or we'll break the door in!"

Straining his ears, Mabry heard somebody within the wagon reply, but could distinguish no words. Then Barker turned to the others. "She says she's got a gun."

"She's lying!"

Boyle picked up the ax and walked to the door. He

balanced the ax, drew it back, and swung hard. As the ax struck there was a heavy concussion within and Boyle sprang back, tripping over the ax and falling. There was a bullet hole in the door on a level with his head.

Mabry hesitated. He could walk in now, but if he were killed in the shoot-out, Healy would be helpless to get the girls back to civilization. He might kill all three, but the odds were against it, and having killed Guilford, they would not submit tamely to capture.

There was no simple solution. At present they were stopped cold, yet there could be little food in the wagon and the women's fuel must be about gone. There were blankets, however, and plenty of clothes. And they could huddle together for warmth.

Carefully he eased back into the trees. At night, that would be the time.

Snow fell, hissing softly. The tracks he left behind were gone. When Mabry got back to the black, the big horse was covered with snow. Mabry went up to him, speaking softly. Suddenly the horse jerked his head up and his ears twitched.

That and the sudden smash of sound were the last things Mabry remembéred.

It was the nudging of the horse that brought him out of it. That and the awful cold.

He felt the horse nudging at his shoulder and whimpering, and then he felt the cold. In all his life he had never known such cold, for there is no cold such as that when the inner heat of the body dissipates itself and the cold penetrates to even the deepest tissues. His body was a thing of ice.

He rolled over and tried to bring his arms under him, but the muscles refused to work. Then he rolled once more and back again. His legs would not function, or his arms, but he could roll, and the rolling made his body prickle with a million tiny needles.

He rolled and rolled, back and forth, and his head

began to throb, and somewhere down inside him there was a birth of pain.

He worked his fingers, and finally, after several attempts, he got to his knees. Feebly he grabbed for the dangling stirrup, but missed. He fell face down on the trampled snow under the horse.

The will to live was too strong. He began to fight, struggling against the cold as against a visible antagonist, knowing death was very, very near.

He had been shot. That much was clear. He had been wounded. He had lost blood. That was against him, for a wounded man has small chance for survival in the cold. And the cold was frightful. It had cut deep, it was within him, robbing his body of its last heat. But he would not let himself die. He got his hands under him again, and he rolled over again, and he got to his knees again.

How long it took him he had no idea. It seemed an endless, bitter struggle. But he got to his knees again and he reached out and drew the stirrup close. He could not grasp it, for his hands were like clubs, useless except for fumbling movements.

He thrust his arm into the stirrup, and using that leverage, he got half way up, then lunged to his full height and fell against the horse.

Leaning there, he thrust his icy hand under the saddle girth, up under the blanket and against the warm belly. He held it there while the patient black waited and snow fell steadily.

He worked his fingers and the blood began to flow again. His hands were still numb, but the fingers moved. He withdrew his hand and grasped the pommel, pulling himself into the saddle and knocking most of the snow away.

The horse was tied. In his cold, numbed brain he remembered that. It was tied to a bush.

He spoke to the horse and it backed slowly. The horse stopped when the reins drew taut, but the branches were brittle with cold and would snap. He backed the horse again and this time the branches snapped off, and he drew the horse's head around and got the reins in his hands.

Then he started the horse, looping the reins around the saddle horn. Where he was to go he had no idea, or what he was to do. He was hurt, and badly. His leg felt stiff and there was pain in him. The cold was a help in some ways. It would keep down the pain and keep him from bleeding too much. Feebly he struck his hands together, then beat his arms in a teamster's warming, swinging them again and again.

Warmth returned a little, and the horse kept moving. The black was going somewhere and Mabry had no choice but to trust him. All around was a tight white world of snow, shutting out all sound and sight.

The wagons would not move. In the place where they had stopped, much snow would have to be moved before they could start even after the storm passed. By driving into the hollow out of the wind, Barker had trapped himself.

Yet Mabry's own plight was desperate. The warmth stirred by movement was the last warmth in his body. His toes might be frozen, and his face might be. It felt like a mask.

He must get to shelter. He must find warmth. He must . . .

A long time later consciousness returned and he was still on the horse and the horse was still walking. Yet he had never actually lost consciousness, only sunk into a half-world where he was neither dead nor alive.

And the snow fell. . . . It fell softly into a cushiony silence, into a world where all was cloaked in white death and where there was no moving thing but the walking horse and the sifting flakes.

## Chapter Nine

THEY WERE HUDDLED around the fire when they heard a low call. Tom Healy lowered his tin plate, suddenly watchful.

All of the others reached for their guns. The call came again and a rider appeared, walking his horse through the falling snow. It was Griffin.

He got down, then brushed snow from his coat. "All right," he said, "it's done. I killed him."

"You got Mabry?" Boyle was skeptical.

Griffin looked up, unfastening his coat, not taking his eyes from Boyle. "I got him. Want to say I didn't?"

Boyle's eyes were ugly. "I'd like to see the body," he said.

"I shot him twice. Once in the body, once in the head."

"You didn't go up to him?" Barker demanded.

"Think I'm crazy? No, I didn't go near him, but I watched him all of ten minutes and he didn't move. If he wasn't dead, then he is now. No man can lie out there and live."

"Good!" Barker's face was hard with satisfaction. "Now we're clear. That's what I wanted to hear!"

He strode across the clearing, striking his fist into his palm. "Now, Healy—"

He broke stride. The log where Healy had been sitting was deserted. There had been a moment when all attention was on the rider and his news. And Tom Healy was learning. He had turned and walked into the night.

Boyle sprang for the brush and the others followed, except for Griffin, who went to the coffeepot. He glanced up from his filled cup and looked at the smoke coming from the wagon of the women, and his lips thinned

71

down. Getting to his feet, he walked around to the door. When he saw the bullet hole, he nodded. "So that's it."

He stood there, sipping his coffee for perhaps a minute, and then he said conversationally, "Mabry's dead. You can give up on him."

There was still no sound from inside. "You got some money in there?" Griffin asked. "Say, about a thousand dollars?"

"And if we do?" Janice asked.

"Might help you."

"You do it," Janice replied. "You'll get paid."

"Cash?"

"Cash. What shall we do?"

"Sit tight."

He smiled to himself as he moved away.

It was cold in the wagon. The fire was very small, barely kept alive by the last few bits of wood and some old clothing.

Dodie raised herself to an elbow. "You haven't that much."

"He doesn't know that," Janice said.

"But when he finds out?"

"By then we may be out of here. Maybe we'll have only one man to deal with."

Maggie coughed, a hoarse, racking cough. Janice turned her head and looked toward the older woman's bunk, but said nothing. In the dark they could only vaguely see outlines, but Janice knew the older woman was very ill.

The continual cold as well as the closeness of the air was doing her no good. Unless she received some warm food and some attention . . . Janice walked the floor of the wagon, three steps each way.

Dodie was quiet. She had said almost nothing since producing the gun. Suddenly she spoke. "I don't believe it. I don't believe he's dead."

"You heard what was said."

"I don't care. I just don't believe it."

Outside, Griffin stood by the fire. He was not a trusting man. He had received half the money for killing Mabry, but did not expect Barker to pay the rest willingly. Mabry was dead now, and Barker had two men to side with him.

Griffin sloshed the coffee in his cup, listening for sounds from the search. Snow continued to fall. This was no time to start anywhere. This was a bad storm and it might get worse. Nor would it be a good time to discuss money with Barker . . . not yet.

When he had Barker alone, that would be the time. And when the storm was over, so he could travel. If he could get the women away, so much the better. He was no man to mess with decent women; he knew the penalty for that in the West.

Wycoff was first to return. He stamped his feet to shake off the snow, then went to the fire and added some sticks he had brought back.

"They won't find him," Wycoff said, "and it makes no difference. By now he's lost, and by morning he'll be dead."

"Prob'ly." Griffin studied Wycoff, thinking of an ally, but decided against opening the subject. Wycoff was a brute. The women would be vastly more important to him than any amount of money.

Boyle? No. Boyle was not to be trusted. He would go it alone. He would watch for his best chance.

Barker and Boyle came in together. "No sign of him. He got into your tracks and by that time you couldn't tell them apart."

"He'll die out there," Boyle said. "He ain't got a chance."

Three quarters of a mile west and stumbling through deepening snow, Healy was panting heavily. Once free of the camp, he had circled to find the horse tracks, thinking they would lead him to Mabry's body.

Griffin had not gone up to Mabry, hence he had not

taken his guns. With those guns he might have a chance, Healy knew.

He had started to run, and had run until pain knifed his side and his breath came in ragged gasps. Then he slowed and for the first time gave thought to being trailed. But it was dark, and by the time they could seriously attempt trailing him, his tracks would be covered with snow. So he slogged along, head down, following the rider's trail.

It was bitter cold. He got out his scarf and tied it across his face. The earlaps on his fur cap were down, and that helped. Yet the tracks were fast filling with snow, and unless he found Mabry soon the trail would be lost.

He reached the end of the tracks suddenly. But where the body should have been lying there was nothing. Man, horse, and guns were gone!

So Mabry was not dead . . . yet there was a dark blotch on the ground not yet covered with snow, a blotch that might be blood.

Mabry was wounded. It was bitter cold and Healy knew no man could last in such cold when he had lost blood and was undoubtedly suffering from shock. A man needed a warm place, care, and treatment. He needed, above all, rest.

Healy was very tired. Today he had worked harder with an ax than he had ever worked before. And he must have run almost a quarter of a mile in deep snow, yet he dared not stop. He turned and followed the tracks of the horse bearing Mabry.

From the time it had taken Griffin to reach camp, and the time it had taken Healy to get to the place where Mabry had been ambushed, Mabry could not have been on the ground for long. Yet in this cold a man could die in a very short time.

Healy did not try to hurry. That was useless now, and he had not the strength for it. Head down to the wind, he pushed on, content to keep putting one foot before the other.

His forehead ached from the cold wind and his face was stiff. There was no place to stop. There was no definite place to go. He could only follow that rapidly vanishing line of tracks.

Twice he fell. Each time he merely got to his feet and walked on.

Pausing at the top of the hill, he listened. Common sense told him there would be no pursuit. Barker would not overestimate his chances of survival and finding him would be nearly impossible.

Somewhere ahead of him a wounded man clung to a wandering horse, but he could not be far ahead, for in such snow a horse could not move much faster than a man. Yet after a time Healy began to realize that the horse was not wandering. He was being ridden or was going by himself toward a definite goal.

The survival of Mabry and himself might well depend on how well he clung to that dwindling line of tracks. They were rapidly becoming only hollows in the snow.

Only movement kept him warm. There was no sound but the hiss of falling snow. He was lost in a white and silent world.

Starting on again, he brought up short against a cliff. Yet almost at once his heart gave a leap. Mabry's horse had stopped here, too.

And for some time. When the horse started on again, the hoofprints were sharp and definite. That horse was only minutes ahead!

Excited, Healy plunged into the snow. He tried running, but fell headlong. Getting to his feet, he realized how close he was to collapse, and knew his only hope was to move on carefully, to conserve his failing energy.

He lost all track of time. He lost all thought of himself. Numbed by cold, he staggered on, keeping the trail

by a sort of blind instinct. He walked as a man in his
sleep, forgetting the existence of everything but the vast
white world in which he lived and moved. He seemed
to be on an endless conveyor belt that carried him on
and on and never ceased to move.

Once, a long time later, he thought he heard a faint
sound.

Head up, he listened. Nothing. He walked on, head
down, moving ahead like a blind, unreasoning automaton.
He brought up suddenly against a solid obstruction. Lifting his head, he found himself against the bars of a pole
corral.

Following the corral bars around, he saw dimly through
falling snow a darker blur. It took shape, became real.
It was a low log house, and at the door stood a horse, and
in the saddle was a man.

It was a man upon whose clothes the snow had caked
and whose head hung on his chest. How he had stayed
in the saddle was a mystery until Healy tried to re-
move him from the horse.

He pounded on the door. No sound. He dropped a hand
to the latch, lifted it, and opened the door.

"Hello!" he shouted. "Anybody home?"

No one answered.

Fumbling then, he got a mitten off a half-frozen hand
and dug into his pocket for matches. His fingers were so
stiff that he had to make several attempts before one
burst into flame.

And the first thing he saw was a half-used candle. His
hand trembled as he held the match to the wick. It
caught, flame mounted, the room became light.

Lifting the candle, he looked around. The cabin was
empty. Before him was a fireplace and on the hearth a
fire had been laid. He used the candle, holding the
flame to the kindling. As it flared up he returned out-
doors and broke the frozen snow from around the stirrup.

Pulling, he found that Mabry's clothes had frozen to

the saddle, and had to be freed by force. He toppled the big man into his arms but was unable to carry him, so he dragged him through the door and into the cabin.

Dragging Mabry closer to the fire, Healy added sticks and built it up until flames crackled and the heat reached out to war against the empty chill of the deserted house.

He got Mabry's coat off, then his boots. He had no experience with frozen men, nor was he sure that Mabry was frozen or even frostbitten, but he began to chafe his feet gently, then warmed the coat at the fire and spread it over his feet. He lifted Mabry's arms and worked them back and forth and around to restore circulation.

There was an ugly tear in Mabry's scalp and his face was covered with dried and frozen blood. Healy hesitated to touch the wound, deciding for the time being to let well enough alone.

With the fire blazing cheerfully and Mabry stretched on a buffalo robe and under blankets, Healy took the candle and walked around the cabin. Obviously it had been in use not many weeks before. In various cans there were dried beans, rice, salt, flour, and coffee.

Shrugging into his coat, he led the patient black horse to the barn. The building was snug and tight, half underground. In a bin he found some ears of corn, and he put them in the feedbox. He wiped the snow from the horse with his hands, then with an old bit of sacking. A couple of moth-eaten blankets hung on nails, and he put them over the horse, forked some hay into the manger, and returned to the house.

Mabry still lay on the floor. The fire burned steadily.

Dull with exhaustion, Healy backed up to a chair and sat down. He would rest. After a while he would make coffee. Outside the snow continued to fall, and the fire ate at the pine knots, and there was no sound within the room but the breathing of the two men. Occasionally a drop of melted snow fell down the chimney into the fire. It was very still.

## Chapter Ten

HEALY AWAKENED with a start and for a minute lay still, trying to orient himself. Slowly he remembered, recalling his arrival and the finding of Mabry.

The big gun fighter lay sprawled on his buffalo robe several feet from the fire. His breathing was heavy, his face flushed and feverish.

Building up the fire, Healy put water in a kettle and hung it over the flames. There was little wood left in the fuel box.

He went to the window. It was growing light and everything was blanketed with snow. All tracks were wiped out. There was small chance of being found, yet while they stayed here, what would happen at the wagons?

He put the thought from his mind. There was nothing he could have done without being armed. His only chance had been to do what he had done, to find Mabry and get a gun. He had the gun now, but not the slightest idea where he was or how to locate the wagons.

Still, the Hole-in-the-Wall was a landmark that must be visible for some distance, and the Wall itself was miles long.

One thing at a time. If he could save Mabry they might have a chance.

When the water was hot he made coffee and then went to work on the wounded man. He took off the short jacket and found the other wound. Mabry had been hit low on the side right above the hipbone, and his side and stomach were caked with blood.

He bathed both wounds, taking great care and much hot water. He felt movement. Looking up, he saw that Mabry's eyes were open.

Mabry looked from Healy to the wound. "How is it?"

"I don't know," Healy admitted. "You've lost a lot of blood. You've got a scalp wound, too."

When he had finished bathing the wounds, he bound them with bandages torn from a clean flour sack.

"Where are we?"

"I don't know that, either." He explained what had happened and how they had reached the cabin.

"Horse came home," Mabry said. "That's got to be it. Bought him in Deadwood from a trapper from over this way. So when the horse found himself close by and without anybody to guide him, he just came home."

"There was a fire laid, though."

"Custom," Mabry said. "Any man who leaves a cabin leaves materials for a fire. Custom in cold country."

At noon Healy found a woodpile in a shed behind the house and brought in several armloads of wood.

"What'll we do?" he asked suddenly.

"Do the girls have a gun?"

"Yes. I didn't know it, but they had one."

Mabry considered that. As long as their food and fuel held out, and if they did not waste ammunition, they could hold Barker off. It was unlikely they had more than one pistol load. Probably five bullets, and one fired. Four left.

Toward night Mabry's fever mounted. He was very weak. During the day he had examined his hands and feet. By some miracle they had not frozen. Yet he would lose some skin on his feet and ankles and his nose would probably peel. He had been luckier than he had any right to be.

Had Healy not found him at the door, he would have eventually fallen or been knocked from the horse to freeze in the snow. He would never have regained consciousness.

Mabry thought it out. They could not be far from the wagons. Several miles, but not too many. Yet he was weak, very weak, and something had to be done at once. Barker would not wait long. He would grow impatient and find some means of getting the girls out of their wagon.

How much had Healy learned? How much could he do?

That he had nerve enough to act was obvious. He had chosen his break and escaped. He had, before that, made his try for the shotgun. He had nerve enough if it was directed right.

"You got to play Indian."

"Me?" Healy shook his head. "I'd never get away with it."

"You've got to. You've got to go back."

Healy would be bucking a stacked deck, yet he might make it if he was lucky . . . and there was no other way.

Pain lay in Mabry's side and his mouth was dry. His skull throbbed heavily. He explained carefully and in detail what Healy must do, and what he would do if he was forced to fight or run. Yet somewhere along the line his mind began to wander and he found himself arguing with himself about Janice.

Vaguely he was aware that Healy was gone, that the Irishman had started out to do something he himself should be doing, but he could not bring his thoughts to focus upon the problem. Before him and through his mind there moved a girl, sometimes with one face and sometimes with another. He kept arguing with Janice and kept seeing Dodie, and the latter's warmth and beauty kept moving between himself and Janice, distracting him and making his carefully thought-out arguments come to nothing.

He told himself in his delirium that he had no business loving any woman, or allowing any woman to love him. He told the image that came to him in his sickness that he would be killed, shot down from behind, or sometime he would draw too slowly. Someone would come along and his gun would misfire, or some Sioux would get a shot at him and not miss.

His life was action, he was of the frontier and for the frontier, he was a man born for a time, and when that time had gone, he would go as the buffalo had gone, and as the Indians were going.

He knew this now as he had always known it, deep in

his subconscious he knew it, and now in his delirium it came back to him with new force.

Before the quiet beauty and the ladylike qualities of Janice Ryan he seemed brutal and uncouth. She was something from the life he had known as a boy, a life long gone now, the life of Virginia before the War between the States. She was hoop skirts and crinoline, she was soft music and a cadence of soft voices. She was a lady. She was something left behind.

Back there along the line of his being there had been a war and he had gone into it from one world and come out of it into another. To him there had not even been ashes, not even memory. The others had tried to cling to the memory, to recall the past. They clung to it with desperate fingers, but he had never been able to see it as anything real. And he had gone West.

He had been only a boy, but a man by virtue of the work he did and the weapon he carried. It had not been far from those days to the XIT and that still, hot morning when he first killed a man without the excuse of war.

He tried to explain this to the shadow figure of Janice, but she kept leaving and Dodie would appear in her place, and somehow there was no explaining to do.

Out in the snow Healy had been doing his own thinking. What did Mabry have in mind? The man was a fighter. He would have known just what to do. But could he, Healy, do it?

He tried to think it out, to plan his moves. Mabry might have gone in to face them down. This Healy knew he could not do. And above all, he must not be killed. He remembered something he had read or heard about military tactics. "The first object of the commander is to keep his striking force intact." And he himself was the striking force.

Tomorrow he might kill a man, or might himself be killed. What would Janice think of him then? It was all very well to talk of not killing, easy to be horrified by it when living in a safe and secure world, but out here it was different.

Nor was there any possibility of aid. There was no law. Nobody knew where they were or had reason to worry about them. They were isolated by distance and the cold, and it was kill or be killed.

Tom Healy was realistic enough to understand that whatever else was done with Janice and Dodie, they would never be allowed to leave the country alive. Their stories, whereever told, would bring sure retribution.

Returning to the house, he put wood on the fire and crawled into his bunk.

At daylight he could see that Mabry was a very sick man. There was little firewood left in the pile behind the house, and the last of Mabry's beef would be used that day. There were a few items of food in the house, but Healy was no cook. Whatever was done he must do.

Thrusting Mabry's extra pistol into his belt, he took up the ax and went out. The snow was knee-deep on the level and he waded through it to the trees in back of the stable. Remembering how far the sound of an ax carried, he hesitated to use it, but there was no alternative.

For an hour he worked steadily. He found the wood brittle in the sharp cold, and he cut up a couple of deadfalls and carried the wood into the house. If Mabry returned to consciousness he would be able to feed the fire.

He tried to put himself in Mabry's place and do what the gun fighter would have done.

Taking the rifle, he went up the ridge east of the house. The wind had an edge like a knife and the hills up there were bare and exposed, without timber and largely swept clean of snow.

Far away to the east he could see the long line of the Wall, which seemed to be no more than seven or eight miles off, yet he was aware of the amazing clarity of the West's air, and that distance could be deceptive.

Well away to the south he could see a notch in the Wall that might be the Hole.

If the wagons started to move, this might well be the route they would take, yet nothing moved anywhere that he could see.

For more than an hour he scouted the country, moving carefully, trying to use the shelter of ridges and tree lines, drawing on his imagination and remembering what he had seen others do, and the casual things Mabry had said, or others. Had he been well, Mabry would have known what to do; as he was not, it was Healy's problem.

Coming from a ravine, he saw a faint trail of smoke in the sky ahead of him. Crouching near a rock, he studied the place of its origin. It was far west of the Hole, almost due south of him, and apparently not over a mile away.

The ravine across the narrow valley was choked with brush but there was a vague game trail along one side, hugging the brush and trees. Along this he made his way. He felt jumpy inside, and knew that where there was smoke there would be men, and at this time those men could scarcely be friends. If it wasn't Barker or his men, it could well be Indians.

Healy was no fool. He had the beginning of wisdom, which was awareness of what he did not know. Yet he must go ahead and trust to luck and what his imagination would provide.

The brush was heavily weighted with snow. Once a rabbit jumped up almost under his feet. He hated the crunch of snow under his boots, fearing it might be heard.

He shifted the rifle to his other hand and worked up the ravine to the top, climbed out and went up the short slope to the crest.

He was just about to peer over the ridge when he heard a shout. Instantly he flattened out on the snow and lay still, listening.

"Can you see it?" The voice was Boyle's.

"Swing left!" That was Barker. "Big rock here!"

He heard the jangle of harness and knew the vans were moving. They had come out of the Hole at last.

Lying near the upthrust of a cluster of boulders, he watched them coming. They were still some distance away, but he could hear every sound in the sharp, clear air.

It was almost noon.

Art Boyle had never liked camping in the Hole. It was the logical route for any traveler going east or west, and evidently he had persuaded Barker to move back into the hills and out of sight. Within a few days, perhaps within hours, all evidence of their presence at the Hole-in-the-Wall would be gone.

Unlikely as it was that any traveler might pass, they were now safe from the risk.

Yet Healy instantly realized there was one thing he must do and could do. He must destroy their confidence. He must let them know they were not secure from discovery. That he, or someone, was still around.

As long as they were watched, or any witnesses remained, they were not safe. Without doubt they were moving back to the hills to accomplish their ambitions once and for all. And once they were back in the ravines and woods and free from discovery, there was only the matter of breaking into the wagons or starving the girls into submission. They might even, and the very thought frightened Healy, set fire to the wagons. Yet they would hesitate to do that without looting them first.

He lifted the rifle. He fired into the snow just ahead of Barker's horse. The rifle leaped in his hands, snow spurted under the horse's hoofs, and the sound went racketing off across the snow-clad hills.

Frightened, the horse leaped forward, then broke into a wild bucking that Barker controlled only after a hard fight. Then he swung the horse over the hill and out of sight. The teams, just now in sight, swung hard around, almost upsetting the vans, and then they lunged into the hollow behind the hill and out of sight. For luck, Healy fired again.

He knew they might very well attempt to locate and kill him, so instantly he slid back down the hill, then moved swiftly into the thick brush. Twisting and winding through it, he made a quarter of a mile before he paused to glance back. There was no evidence of any pursuit.

At least, Barker now knew his problem was not simple. He must find and kill Healy or abandon his plan, and this he would not do. They would know the shot had been fired by no Indian, for Healy knew enough of the West by this time to know that an Indian had no ammunition to waste. When he shot, he shot to kill.

Returning to the cabin, he found Mabry conscious and sitting up, his pistol gripped in his hand and the muzzle on the door.

Healy explained what he had done as he got out of his coat. "Think they'll come here?"

"Could be. Won't do any harm," Mabry added, "taking that shot at them." He lay back on the bed, relaxing his grip on the pistol. "I'm not much use to you."

Healy rubbed his hands down his pants. Anything could happen now . . . and Janice was out there. If they hurt her . . . He knew suddenly how it was that a man could kill.

## Chapter Eleven

Janice awakened suddenly with Dodie's hand upon her shoulder. Outside she could hear a confused sound of voices, and the air was cool inside the wagon. They were, she remembered, almost out of fuel.

"We've stopped," Dodie whispered.

Janice lay still, staring up into the half-light inside the wagon, facing the fact that they were still trapped.

There was no longer any food in the wagon, and their only water had been from snow scraped off the roof by opening the window and reaching an arm through to the top. As the small window was close under the eaves, it was simple enough. Yet it was little water for three women.

From the sound of the hoarse breathing from the opposite bunk, Janice knew that Maggie was no better. If anything, she sounded worse.

The decision to move had been Barker's. Once he had assurance that Mabry was dead, they had begun the back-breaking job of getting the wagons out of the Hole.

It had been a brutal job, digging out around the wagons, then cutting through the snowdrift and packing down snow to get the wagons out. And they had to use both teams on each wagon to get them out of the hollow. Once they were on open ground, the move had gone well, until those startling and unexplained shots from nowhere.

Yet no attack followed . . . only silence.

"If that was Healy," Boyle said, "he'll starve out there. Or he'll get careless and come too close."

"Mabry wouldn't have wasted his lead," Barker said thoughtfully. "He'd shoot to kill."

"Mabry's dead," Griffin repeated patiently.

Boyle looked up, sneering.

Griffin's feet moved apart, his eyes widened a little, and with his left hand he slowly unbuttoned his coat.

Boyle's eyes held on Griffin's. The sly egotism of the man had been jolted. His face turned a sickly gray and his fear was almost tangible.

Suddenly alert, Barker turned on Griffin. "Grif," he said quickly, "did you see any Indian tracks?"

Griffin let his eyes hold Boyle's. "Couple of times. Six in a bunch once. All bucks."

Art Boyle sat very quiet. The slightest wrong move or word could force him to grab for his gun . . . and it was obvious that he could not beat Griffin.

Sullenly Barker sat his saddle and reviewed the situation, liking none of it. Tom Healy had, somewhere in these wagons, fifteen thousand in gold, the money he was carrying to Maguire, or so his informant in the bank had told him. To get that money had seemed very simple.

Barker had wanted to go back to that little group of towns, Bannock, Alder Gulch, and Virginia City. Some years had passed and most of the old vigilante crowd had gone away. If anybody remained who knew he had been one of the Plummer crowd, nobody could prove it. Moreover, old passions had died, and the vigilante crowd would not be so eager to move against a man for old crimes.

It had seemed a simple thing to take the Healy party out, kill the men, enjoy the women, and then burn the wagons and bury the bodies, moving on to the old mining camps at the Gulch.

A traveling show was always moving anyway, and nobody would be surprised that they were gone. It was probable that months would pass before any inquiries could be made. And he could always say they paid him off and went their own way.

Once established back in the Gulch, he could open a saloon, or buy one, and slowly rebuild some of the old gang. The mines were slowing down, and there would be less people to rob, but less danger, also.

The first flaw in the picture had been the arrival of
King Mabry.

Not even Boyle knew that Barker himself was a gunman, but good as he was, Barker was not sure he could
beat King Mabry, nor had he any urge to try. He was
looking for the sure things, and robbing Healy had seemed
without risk.

Yet his entire plan demanded that it be done without
leaving witnesses. Travelers took the old Bozeman Trail
to Montana up the valley of the Powder, or went west
along the trail from Fort Laramie to Salt Lake if they
were bound for California. The overland route that he
had chosen to take them to Alder Gulch would ordinarily
be deserted . . . and then his plans went awry at the discovery of the hoof tracks.

Suspecting that somehow Mabry had missed them and
gone on through the Hole-in-the-Wall, Barker had waited
for Griffin to accomplish his mission. And the wild country
beyond the Wall was the ideal place for what he planned
to do.

Already a few outlaws were beginning to use that country as a haven, and a man who intended to kill three wom-
en had better be sure it was not known.

Then everything had gone wrong at once. The unexpected gun in the girls' wagon, then the escape of Healy.
Unable to find the money in Healy's wagon, Barker became sure it was in the wagon with the girls.

With the wagons hauled away from the trail through
the Hole and hidden away up Red Creek Canyon, with
Mabry dead and Healy probably dying, they could act.
They would destroy the wagons, scatter the ashes. And as
for the girls . . . in a few days they could kill them, too.

Barker was a cold-blooded, matter-of-fact man. Plummer's final failure at the Gulch and Virginia City had been
a warning. And even while the first vigilante hanging,
that of George Ives, was in progress, Barker had taken
a quick road out of the country.

And in the years that followed he had guarded himself

well, and worked always with care. He wanted to take
no chances. He had seen what had happened in Virginia
City when almost to a man his old comrades had been
wiped out. A Western community might stand for a lot,
but when it drew a line, it was drawn hard and fast and
certain.

Until the girls had been molested, there was always a
retreat, but that was the point of no return. The killing
of Doc Guilford could be alibied. Doc had a gun, and
he had drawn it; Wycoff had been wounded. Even the
girls and Healy must admit that. So there was still a way
out.

The sudden shots from the hilltop angered and frightened him.

Healy was alive and he had a weapon. And until Healy
was certainly dead, they dared not proceed with the rest of
the plan. There must be none to report what had happened. And when he thought that, Barker was also thinking of Griffin.

The first order of business was to hunt down Healy and
kill him. He said as much.

"That's your business," Griffin told him. "You go ahead
with it."

"What's that mean?"

"I've done my job. I've no part of this." He paused
briefly. "And I'm not asking any share."

Barker hesitated. That was true enough, and somebody
must guard the wagons.

"All right, Boyle can come with me. Two of us should
be enough."

Janice watched the men saddling their horses. Griffin
was remaining behind, but what could Griffin do with
Wycoff still around? And there was something about the
sullen brutality of Wycoff that she feared even more than
Barker.

Gently she touched Maggie's brow. It was so hot that
she was frightened.

Dodie saw her expression. "We've got to get help for her," Dodie said. "We've got to get out. She should have some warm soup."

Now, with Griffin here, they might get help. The man was a killer, she knew. Yet she had heard of men of his kind. She had seen the killing fury that obsessed such men, but even the worst men in the West might respect a good woman. This must be true of Griffin. It had to be true.

Standing at the door, she watched the riders go back down the trail the way they had come. From her bed she picked up the gun.

"I'll go." Dodie got up quickly. "You stand by the door with the gun."

"Don't get out of sight."

The sound of the opening door turned both men. Janice saw the sudden shine of animal fever in Wycoff's eyes. He took a half step forward.

Janice stepped into the doorway, holding the gun in plain sight. "Mr. Griffin, we've a sick woman in here. She needs warm food, and I'm afraid she has pneumonia."

Griffin's lean face was grave. He looked at her out of gray, cold eyes and nodded. "Of course. We'll make her some broth."

Wycoff said something under his breath and Griffin turned on him sharply. From Wycoff's reaction, Janice knew that whatever Griffin had said angered him.

Griffin turned back to her, but kept his eyes on Wycoff as he spoke. "Wait," he said. "I'll make the soup."

"I can make it." Dodie stepped past Janice, a small kettle in her hand. "If you'll give me what I need."

Wycoff backed off a step, watching Dodie. He glanced from her to Griffin and touched his tongue to his lips. When he glanced at the wagon Janice held her gun on him. He backed up and sat down.

Dodie went to the fire, accepted meat and barley from Griffin, and went to work. From time to time she glanced at Wycoff.

Janice saw that the teamster was staring hungrily at Dodie as she worked, but the threat of the gun in the doorway held him back. And Dodie was careful never to come between the gun and Wycoff. She worked swiftly, but with no lost motion.

When the soup was ready, Griffin gestured at the coffeepot. "Take that, too. You and Miss Ryan could use some coffee, I expect."

Janice saw Wycoff get to his feet and turn away. He walked slowly, and Griffin turned instantly to watch him. Wycoff's right hand was carried a little high, his elbow bent. Griffin's lips thinned down.

"Try it," he said. "I'll kill you if you do."

Wycoff turned carefully, letting his arm straighten. When he completed his turn he was smiling. "Sure. I can wait." He walked back to the fire and sat down. "Don't know Barker very well, do you?" He nodded toward Griffin's gun. "He's better with one of those than you are. He's better, maybe, than Mabry. Seen him at Rattlesnake Ranch, where the Plummer gang used to hang out. Plummer could beat him, but not all the time. I seen him empty a gun into a post in no more'n a second."

"Did the post have a gun?"

Wycoff's lips thinned down at the retort, but he made no further comment.

Dodie hurried back to the wagon then and Janice closed the door.

Dodie fed Maggie her soup. The older woman was conscious and seemed aware of their surroundings. She looked up at Dodie. "Are we still here?"

"Yes."

"I wish that man with the guns would show up. I had faith in him."

"Yes." Dodie looked at Janice. "I think he was in love with you."

"Oh, no!" she protested.

"If you had asked him, he would have come with us."

"Did you ask him?"

"He wouldn't have come for me," Dodie said quietly, "but if he had asked me, I would have gone with him."

"But he's a killer!"

"I wish we had him here now," Dodie said. "I wish we did."

Suppose, Janice thought, she had asked him? It was too late to think of that now and there had been no reason to ask him, only . . . she knew that Tom had secretly wanted him to come, respecting his experience. Yet if what Griffin had said was true, he must have followed them.

"I scarcely talked to him!" she said.

"I didn't talk to him at all," Dodie replied quietly. "But I would have gone with him."

Dodie had made enough soup for all three, and now Janice and Dodie took their plates and began to eat. Janice was thinking back to the moment when she had first seen Mabry in the stage station, how her step had faltered, and how he glanced at her quickly, and then went on by, a big, brown-faced man with wide shoulders. Not really good-looking, but strong, so very strong. Her face flushed a little at the thought. She couldn't recall ever before having seen a man who was so—so *male*.

Yet it was not only that. There was a thoughtfulness in him, a consideration for others, a sense of delicacy. He had hesitated to join them at the table, and only when they insisted had he come.

What *was* love, anyway? Who could say how it happened? Did it come only of long association? Or did it come quickly, sharply, like a pain or a shaft of sunlight through clouds?

"I think," Dodie said quietly, "you're in love with him, too!"

## Chapter Twelve

KING MABRY opened his eyes to the shadowed light of late evening. Turning on his side, he glanced around. Healy was gone.

The room was cool, the fire burned down to coals, glowing here and there.

Mabry eased himself out of bed and tried his strength by standing. Shakily he moved to the fireplace. There was wood in the bin, and he built up the fire. Obviously Healy had been gone for some time.

When the fire was blazing again he looked around, found the coffeepot, and put it on the fire with fresh coffee. Surprisingly, despite his weakness, he felt good.

After examining his wounds, he dressed, taking his time and stopping to rest. He was very thirsty and he drank several gourds of water. When the coffee was ready he filled a cup and drank it, black and scalding.

Healy had been gone too long. Mabry belted on his remaining gun and banked the fire carefully. He was restless from confinement but knew his strength would allow only limited movement.

He got into his coat and opened the door, inhaling deeply of the crisp, cold air. It was like drinking deep of a thinner, colder, purer water.

Outside was snow, only snow. Healy's tracks led around the house and he easily picked out the most recent ones. He started to follow, then pulled up short.

Four Indians had stopped their horses on the slope near the barn and were looking toward the house. All were young, and they looked mean and tough.

Mabry remained where he was, at the corner of the house. Three of the Indians had Winchesters and he had only his .44, but there was a slit inside his buffalo-coat pocket that enabled him to reach through and draw the gun under cover of the coat.

The Indians were wrapped in moth-eaten blankets and two wore old government-issue Army jackets. They started down the slope, but one hung back, arguing angrily.

One dismounted and started for the door of the barn, and Mabry knew it was time to make a move or lose a horse. He stepped past the corner of the house and loosened the loops around the buttons of his coat with his left hand. He had taken three steps before they saw him.

"How," Mabry said, and waited.

These were renegade Sioux, and if trouble started they would be tough to handle. The Indian who had hung back he discounted. This Indian was older, his blanket looked better, and he had a shrewd look about him.

"Where squaw?" The Indian on the ground spoke first.

"No squaw," Mabry said. "Just one horse and one gun."

One of the mounted Indians grunted and the one on the ground started to open the barn door.

"Lay off that!" Mabry started forward quickly, and as he moved the mounted Indian lifted his rifle. Turning on the ball of his foot, Mabry shot through the opening of his coat, and the Indian let go of his rifle and fell forward over his horse's neck and into the snow.

The unexpectedness of it stopped them. They had seen no gun, and the white man seemed to be alone. They looked from the dead Indian to Mabry, and there was a smell of gun smoke in the air.

Then the Indian who had not wanted trouble turned his pony and started to ride away. The remaining mounted man started to follow, but the Indian on the ground started to pick up the fallen Winchester. As he reached for it, a bullet kicked up snow in his face and a rifle report slapped hard against the hills.

"Leave that!" Mabry shouted. "Get going!"

The Sioux said something bitter and swung to his pony's

back. He turned the pony, and, his face dark with anger, he shouted at Mabry again.

When they were out of sight, Mabry crossed to the Winchester and picked it up. It was newer than his own, and carved into the stock were the initials H.S. Stolen from some white man, or taken from a body.

Tom Healy came down off the ridge with the rifle in his hands. "Thought I'd let 'em know you weren't alone."

"Good man."

"Those Indians are heading right for the wagons," Healy said anxiously. "And there's more of them close by."

The Indian pony stood a few yards away, near the dead brave. They had not even offered to carry him away, which was additional evidence that they were renegades, outlawed by the tribe, probably, as well as by the whites.

The pony had an old brand on his shoulder, and he shied slightly when Mabry walked to him. "Ride this one," he said. "I'll saddle up."

His head was aching with a dull, persistent throb, and his side bothered him, but he felt good. Yet he would have little endurance . . . that he must remember.

They were astride the horses and moving when the first shot sounded. It was over in the woods to the east of them, and it was followed by an outburst of firing. Swinging his horse, Mabry put the black down the trail at a hard run.

Just as he cleared the crest he heard another burst of firing, then a scream.

The two vans were drawn up as Healy had said, but now a man lay sprawled over a log, his head split open and his skull showing the raw red wound where a scalp had been jerked free.

The three Indians who had ridden from the cabin had been joined by four others. Three of them struggled with Janice at the door of the van. A white man lying on the ground tried to lift himself for a shot, but an Indian fired first and the man was slammed back to the earth.

From within the van there was a heavy report. Ignoring the Indians fighting with Janice, Mabry dropped to one knee as he slid from his horse. He took a careful breath, let it out, and squeezed off his shot.

An Indian sprang suddenly forward. His body slammed hard against the side of the van, then fell back. Instantly Mabry shifted his rifle to another Indian and fired.

One of those near Janice sprang away and grabbed at his rifle, which lay against a log. Healy shot and the Indian stumbled, then started forward again.

But Healy had shot from the back of his horse and now the pony went charging down the hill into the middle of the wild scramble around the vans.

Mabry grabbed at the pommel as the black started, felt a tearing pain in his wounded side, and then was in the saddle and riding low like an Indian.

Three Sioux were down and the others running. One took a snap shot and Mabry heard the sound of the bullet. He fired across the saddle, holding his rifle with one hand. Then he fired again, and the Indian went down.

He swung the black and looked back at the vans. Healy was on the ground and fighting with an Indian. Dodie had come out of the wagon with a Colt in her hand, but Janice had been thrown across a pony and an Indian was mounted behind her.

The black was rested and corn-fed. Moreover, he liked to run. Mabry jumped him into a lunging run, angling across the course of the Sioux. As Mabry came up on him the Sioux threw Janice from him into a drift and swung to meet Mabry. As they came abreast, the lean, savage-faced Indian threw himself from his horse and hit Mabry. They went off the running horse into the snow.

The Sioux struck viciously with his knife but the blade caught in Mabry's buffalo coat. Mabry caught the Indian's greasy hair and jerked his face down to meet the upward smash of Mabry's skull in the crushing "Liverpool kiss" known to water-front and rough-and-tumble fighters. The brave fell back, his face streaming blood from a broken nose and smashed lips.

Heedless of the knife, Mabry swung. It was a wide swing and should not have landed, but it did. The Sioux went down, rolled over, and came up, his face a smear of blood. He threw himself at Mabry, his knife held low, cutting edge up. Mabry slapped the knife wrist aside to deflect the point, then caught the arm and threw the Indian over his hip, breaking his arm.

The brave hit hard but came up again, his knife arm askew, and grabbed for his fallen rifle. Mabry shot him from the hip with his .44 and the Indian stumbled three steps forward and slid on his face in the snow.

Janice was on her knees, her hair fallen around her shoulders, her face haggard, her dress ripped.

His heart pounding wildly, Mabry spun around, his gun ready to chop down any further attackers. But what Indians remained alive were gone.

He walked over and dropped beside Janice. With a ragged sob, she fell into his arms. He held her, looking past her to the wagons.

Dodie stood near them, shading her eyes toward them. Slow smoke lifted from the fire. There was the quiet of a fading winter afternoon, crisp and cold. The sky was gray, with only the dark line of crouching trees to offer relief.

Singularly, nowhere was there violence. It had come, smashing with its sudden horror, and then was gone. Gently Mabry lifted the sobbing girl to her feet.

Walking slowly to his horse, he retrieved his rifle from the snow. He could feel the wetness of blood inside his clothes, and the ache in his head beat heavily.

At the wagons Dodie waited for them. Her face was white and still. "There were seven," she said. "They took the horses."

Two Indians lay near the wagons. One of them sprawled at the foot of the step to the door. Mabry glanced at the body. This Indian had been shot at point-blank range and his chest was covered with powder burns. Mabry glanced thoughtfully at Dodie, who still held the Colt.

The man with his head split open was Wycoff. The

other man was Griffin. He was fairly riddled with bullets.

"He killed another one, I think," Dodie said, "up under the trees. They came so suddenly, we—"

"I know," Mabry said. "Get what food there is. We've got to get away from here. They'll be back."

"After *that?*" Healy asked.

"These were renegades, without squaws. They'll be back."

Janice straightened, drawing away from him. With one hand she pushed her hair back. "I'm sorry," she said. "I . . . It was just . . ."

"Don't think about it. Get ready to move."

He walked to the Indian at the step and, taking him by the heel, dragged him away. His blood made a red streak on the trampled snow and Janice turned her face away.

Slowly, holding an elbow against his bad side, Mabry picked up the scattered weapons. Two Indian rifles and the rifle Wycoff had carried. Griffin's horse and rifle were gone, but Mabry unbuckled the cartridge belt and took the Colt. The Indian pony that Healy had ridden was gone too.

"We *can't* go," Janice protested. "Maggie's sick. She's very sick."

"I'm sorry." Mabry's voice was harsh from his own pain. "She'll have to go. We can't defend this place. We surprised them once. Next time they won't be surprised."

Tom Healy came up quietly and took Janice by the arm. "You get the food. I'll help Dodie with Maggie."

Janice hesitated. "You can't bring her out like this! You can't let her see those—those bodies."

Mabry turned impatiently. Every minute counted and his own weakness was growing. There was at least a chance at the cabin, which was strong and well built.

"She'll have to stand it," he replied sharply. "I haven't time to conduct a funeral. Get her wrapped up and let's get going!"

Janice stared at him, her eyes revealing her contempt. She turned abruptly away.

Mabry looked to the hills. He felt sick and empty. He knew there were more Indians around. And he knew they would be coming back.

They would be coming back, and they were just two men, with three women, one too ill to travel.

## Chapter Thirteen

WITH JANICE on one side and Mabry on the other they held the sick woman upon the horse. Maggie seemed only vaguely conscious of what was happening, and Mabry was worried. The sooner they got her into a house and in bed, the better.

Behind the saddle the black was piled high with blankets and quilts from the vans. Upon the Indian pony were supplies and the gold intended for Maguire in Butte.

Dodie walked ahead, carrying the shotgun. Suddenly she stopped, hesitated a moment, and then called, "King?"

Healy took his place beside the horse and Mabry walked up to Dodie. By now it was dark, and the sky was heavily overcast.

"I smell smoke."

Mabry lifted his head, testing the air. It was smoke, all right. And there was a smell he did not like. It was not merely wood smoke.

Telling her to stay with the others and to bring them on carefully, he went on ahead. When he had gone several hundred yards, he stopped again. His imagination had reached ahead and he already knew what he would see. Below him in the darkness a dozen small red eyes winked at the night.

They were all that remained of the fire that had destroyed the cabin.

Gone . . . and the barn also.

Alone in the darkness on the hill, he knew he faced his most desperate hour. For himself it was a small problem, not more than he had often faced. For the others, and particularly the sick woman, it was a matter of life or death.

He did not now think of Barker, long absent from his

thoughts. He no longer thought of the Indians who would soon be seeking out their trail.

He thought only of the three women, who must have shelter, and especially of the sick woman, who must have care, rest, and good food.

Behind him they were coming on, trusting in him. To Janice he was a brute, a savage. It was in her eyes whenever she looked at him. He had saved them, yes. But only by killing and destruction, and she believed him capable of nothing else.

And was he?

Gloomily he stared at the dying embers. There was no time to think of that now. The sick woman could go little farther.

This was new country to him, but like all mountain men and plainsmen, he looked carefully at a country when he rode across it. Riding out that day with Healy, he had noticed a brush-choked ravine.

He walked back to meet them, explaining the situation without holding back anything. "We won't go near the place," he added. "There's a ravine cuts back to the north."

Indians might steal horses by night, but they had little liking for night fighting. But that was not true of Barker, if he had not himself been slain.

The ravine seemed filled with brush, but there was a game trail along one edge. Mabry led the way, and after a few hundred yards the brush thinned out and there were more trees, poplars with more and more evergreens and occasional clumps of aspens. Suddenly he saw what he wanted, a thick grove of young aspens, most of them no more than an inch thick.

Cutting boughs from a pine that stood near the aspens, he made a quick bed on the snow. Atop it he placed a buffalo robe and blankets. Then gently he lifted Maggie from the horse and placed her on the bed.

Then he went into the grove. With the ax brought from the wagons he cut off a dozen or more trees right at ground level. When he had cleared a space some ten feet in diameter he jumped and caught a young tree as high as he could reach. Then, pulling on its branches, he bent the top over. While Dodie held it in place, he bent down another from the opposite side and lashed them together with a piggin string from his saddle. He did the same thing with two other trees at right angles to the first two. Then he pulled down others and tied them all at the center until he had a domelike frame, rooted in the ground.

Janice came to watch, and seeing him weaving evergreen boughs into the framework, she pitched in to help. There were a number of two-year-old pines on the slope of the hill behind the aspens. With Dodie, Janice, and Healy helping, the hut was soon covered and tight. He left a space near the top of the dome for the escape of smoke.

Inside they made beds of evergreen boughs, taking care to strip none of the trees, but to take only a few boughs from each. When the bed inside was ready, Mabry picked Maggie from the ground and carried her inside. Then he made a windscreen for the horses by weaving boughs into the thick brush.

When a fire was going, he circled the outside, looking for any sign of light. Nothing was visible. By using dry wood, smoke could almost be eliminated, and by day it would be somewhat scattered and broken by the branches of the trees overhead.

The wind was rising and there was a smell of snow in the air. And snow at this time would be a godsend, wiping out their trail and covering the shelter with a thick, warm blanket.

Janice sat by the fire, staring into the red coals. When she saw Mabry step back inside the shelter, she asked, "What will we do?"

"Wait. All we can do."

The firelight flickered against the dark, weaving strange

patterns on the walls of their shelter. Maggie stirred restlessly in her sleep, muttering a little. Fragments of lines
spoken long ago, the name of a man whispered lonesome-
ly, longingly.

"Will they come back?"

"They'll come. They know we're only a few."

Janice sat silent, unable to forget how he had fought
with that Indian. He had been welcome, he had saved
her from horror and misery, and yet there had been
something shocking and terrible in the way he fought.
He seemed to go berserk in battle; he forgot his wounds
and everything but killing. At first he had been cool and
methodical. She had glimpsed him on the ridge, firing
from his knee, and then during the fight his face had been
strained, brutal, utterly fierce. What could make a man
like that?

He moved suddenly, putting some small sticks on the
fire, and then firelight flickered on his moving rifle barrel, there was an instant of cold air, and he was outside
in the snow again.

Had he heard something? Or was he just being careful? She glanced across the fire at Healy. He was lying
down, his blankets around him. She felt a sudden desire
to reach out and touch him. He was so lost here. . . . Yet
he had gone into that fight with no thought of himself,
and he had managed to protect them and stay alive.

She wrapped herself in some blankets and was almost
asleep when Mabry returned. There was no sound, but
the blanket curtain at the doorway moved and then he
was inside, huddled over the fire.

Janice believed she was the only one awake, but Dodie's
hand reached out and moved the coffeepot toward him.
Janice felt a little twinge of irritation, and burrowed
deeper into her bed. Yet neither of them spoke.

Outside the wind was rising, and she saw snowflakes
melting from his sleeve when he poured coffee. Inside the
shelter the acrid bite of the smoke made her eyes smart,
but it was warm here, and she slept. . . .

She awakened suddenly in the first cold light of breaking day. Only a spot of gray showed where the smoke hole was. Mabry was on his knees by the fire, coaxing it to flame. Then he reached outside and scooped fresh, clean snow into the kettle, and put it on a rock close to the fire.

She lay still in the vague light, watching him. She was remembering what Dodie had said, that she loved this man. How silly!

She could never love such a man. He was cruel and a brute. Take the way he spoke of Maggie yesterday. Of course, they probably did have to move, but still . . .

His face was like well-tanned leather in the firelight. He wore a blue wool shirt tucked into his pants, and now he was pulling a fringed buckskin hunting shirt over it.

He got up in one lithe, easy movement. She thought she had never seen a man whose muscular co-ordination was so flawless. He went out the door, and when he was gone she got out from her own bed and went to Maggie.

And then she saw that Maggie was covered with Mabry's buffalo coat. Sometime during the night he must have got up and spread the coat over her. His own coat.

Janice went to the packs and began getting out food for a meal. His action puzzled her, making no part of the man she was creating in her mind.

When he had been gone almost an hour he returned suddenly with two good-sized rabbits and some slender branches. He split the branches with his knife and took out the pith. "Add it to the soup," he whispered.

She looked at it doubtfully, then put it into the pot.

"You stay out here," he said, "you'll eat everything. And be glad to get it." He added sticks to the fire, then looked at her quizzically. "Panther meat—now, that's best of all."

"Cat?" She looked to see if he was serious. "Surely you wouldn't—"

"Sure I would. And I have. Mountain men prefer it to venison or bear meat."

Dodie turned over and sat up, blinking like a sleepy child. "It's warmer."

"Colder," Mabry said, "only we're snowed in. Heavy fall last night, and if anybody can see this place at all, it'll look like an igloo."

Maggie opened her eyes and looked around. For the first time in many hours she seemed perfectly rational. "Where are we?" she whispered.

"It's all right, ma'am," King Mabry said. "Just rest easy."

She looked up at the shelter of boughs. The air in the place was heavy with the smell of wood smoke and cooking, but fresher than it had ever been in the van.

"You're a good man," Maggie said. "A good man."

Obviously embarrassed, Mabry turned and began feeding sticks into the fire.

After they had eaten, Mabry lay down, pulled his blankets over him, and slept. He breathed heavily and for the first time seemed to relax completely.

Janice stared down at him, torn by a strange mixture of feelings. There was something . . . yet . . .

"Like I told you," Dodie said, "you're in love with him."

## Chapter Fourteen

JANICE LOOKED quickly to see if Mabry had heard, but he was asleep, breathing easily. She was confused, and nothing seemed right to her, but nothing that happened here could happen in the well-ordered world she had left behind.

"I couldn't love him. He's killed men."

Dodie was fixing her hair. She glanced obliquely at Janice. "Suppose Wycoff had tried to get into the van. Suppose you had shot him. Then you'd have killed a man, too."

"But that's different!"

"Is it?"

Dodie worked with her hair in silence, then studied herself in the tiny glass she held. "Where do you think that gun came from?"

"The gun?"

"The one I had. I got it from my father. It was taken from his body after he was killed in Colorado."

"I should think you'd hate guns!"

"Out here a gun is a tool. Men use them when they have to. I know what King Mabry is like because my father was like that." Dodie touched her hair lightly here and there. "Where there's no law, all the strength can't be left in the hands of the lawless, so good men use guns, too."

Maggie had been listening. "That's uncommonly good sense. Hate to think where we'd all be if it wasn't for him."

Janice turned to her, surprised. "We didn't think you knew!"

"I heard it all. He's a man, that one. I just wish I was young again."

And then for a long time nothing was said and there was only the crackle of the fire. Janice opened the curtain to create a draft that would draw more smoke out at the top.

Cold branches rubbed their fingers together, and in his sleep King Mabry muttered, then lay quiet.

Once, sitting over the fire, Janice heard Healy singing softly . . . a singing Irishman with a heart too big for him.

Occasionally a drop of water fell from the dome as snow melted on the underside of the thick blanket now covering them. It was warm and comfortable within the shelter.

King Mabry awakened to silence. He lay still, thinking it out. Janice put wood on the fire, but Dodie was sleeping. Janice sat by the fire, lost in thought. Making no sound, he watched her for a time, then looked up at the roof.

They had to get out of here. Yet travel, even without a sick woman, would be tough in this weather. Their best bet was to wait out the storm. They were somewhere on the Red Fork of the Powder, that much he knew. The Middle Fork must be south of them.

This was new country for him, but the trapper from whom he bought the black horse had talked a lot about the country, and Mabry was a good listener. There were no maps, and men learned about a country from others who had been there, and men became skillful at description and at recognizing landmarks.

Once they were started, their best bet was to get into the valley of the Big Horn and follow it north into Montana. There would be water and fuel along the river, and they could keep to the hills by day, coming down to get water at night. They had at least a fifty-fifty chance of getting into Montana, and, if their luck held, to some settlement.

Aside from the ever present danger from Indians, there

was Barker. Barker might take what money he had and light out. Yet he must have known about the gold Healy was carrying, and he knew he dared never appear in any Montana camp once this story got out.

Yet Barker was a tough man, not at all the sort to give up easily. Art Boyle would be dangerous only as long as he was with Barker, or if you turned your back on him.

Mabry swung his feet from under the blankets. Then he picked up his fur cap and put it on. He looked at Janice, his brow furrowing.

"Got to leave you for a while. I should be back in a couple of hours, but if I'm not, stay close to this shelter until the storm's over. Always keep a good landmark in sight, and remember the fewer tracks you make, the smaller the chance you'll be found."

He pointed down the ravine. "After I caught those rabbits I set the snares again. There should be a couple more soon. The first one is down the draw about fifty yards under some low brush near a cedar. There's another about the same distance farther along.

"You won't have to hunt wood. Not more than twenty yards down the draw there's a pile of drift around an old deadfall."

"You sound . . . How long will you be gone?"

"Couple of hours, like I said. That's if everything goes well. I might have bad luck and run into some Sioux." He began to clean his rifle. "If the weather breaks good and I'm not back, start out. But you best just wait and let Maggie get well. Or better. That way," he gestured toward the brush, "is safe. Nobody can get to you without plenty of noise. You'll have to watch the slope past the cottonwoods, and I'd suggest you put some brush among the aspens, if you have to stay. When you go out, go through the grove, and don't use the same way twice.

"You've guns enough and ammunition enough, so just sit tight."

"Why are you going, then?"

"Food. I got to rustle some grub. There's five here, and

we have to eat. I've got to go some ways off because I don't want to shoot close by. Of course, I might find some sage hens. A man can kill them with a stick in this snow."

Outside, he led the black horse through the grove and mounted. Then, brushing the edge of the undergrowth to conceal his tracks wherever possible, he went up the draw.

For two hours he rode, scouting the country. Where the wagons had been there were now only ashes. That had to be Barker's work. He found no Indian sign, evidence in itself that they were too smart to travel in bad weather. He found a trail where several buffaloes had drifted along beside a frozen stream, and then he found fresh deer tracks and places where the animals had pawed through the snow to get at the grass underneath.

He killed a sage hen, riding it down in the snow and killing it with a blow from his rifle. That night he camped some five miles from the shelter where the girls and Healy waited. At daybreak, after eating most of the sage hen, he started out again.

Just before noon, in a deep hollow in the hills, he killed a buck. He was riding upwind through the soft snow when he saw movement. He drew rein and waited, his Winchester lifted. The buck came out of the trees and stopped, his head half turned. Mabry dropped him in his tracks with a neck shot.

He made quick work of cutting up his kill. It was a cold job at best, and he was glad to be back in the saddle and moving. Returning, he used every means he could to confuse his trail. It was spitting snow again, so there was hope that his tracks would soon be covered.

Coming up the draw and holding close to the edge of the brush, he saw movement ahead of him.

He lifted his rifle, then caught a glint of sunlight on auburn hair and lowered the rifle. He walked his horse closer and stopped. It was Dodie, and she was taking a rabbit from a snare. Expertly she killed the rabbit with a blow behind the neck.

"You do that like you know how."

She straightened up and smiled at him. "I do. I used to trap them when I was ten years old. I was a tomboy, I'm afraid."

He looked at her and swung down from his horse. "No need to be afraid now. You're no tomboy."

"No . . . I'm not."

He kicked his feet against the ground to warm them. "Everything all right?"

"Yes. Tom was going to do this, but he's been getting wood." She paused. "I see you got a deer."

"Few miles back." He was making talk, not knowing exactly why, except that it was easy to talk to this girl. It was never easy to talk to Janice. Somehow the words just would not come. "It's good country here. I'd like to come back sometime. Lots of game, and this buffalo grass is good fodder all year round."

"Why don't you?" Dodie had come closer to him. She shivered a little. "It's beautiful, really beautiful."

"Lonely country. No neighbors around."

"Who needs neighbors? It's good country for you, King. By the time you had neighbors, people would have forgotten."

She reached up, putting the rabbit behind the saddle with the venison. Then she turned and faced him, her back to the horse, leaning back a little, but very close.

"If a woman really wanted a man she would go to any country with him."

Mabry looked at her and smiled a little. "What do you know about wanting a man?"

"Enough. How much does a girl have to know?"

She looked up at him, eyes teasing and impudent. Deliberately she reached up to brush snow from his shoulder, and then she was in his arms. Afterward he never knew whether he had done it or if she had. She came against him quickly, taking his coat lapels in her hands, her face lifted to his. With a sudden gust of passion he caught her to him, his lips crushing the softness of hers, her body molding itself against his, even through the thickness of their clothing.

One hand slipped around his neck and caught fiercely at the hair on the back of his head. Breathlessly they clung to each other; then Mabry broke loose. He drew back, staring at her and brushing his lips with the back of his hand.

"That's no good," he said. "I'm sorry."

Coolly she lifted a hand and brushed her hair back in place. Her breasts lifted with her breathing. "Sorry? Why?"

"You're just a kid."

She laughed at him. "Did I feel like a kid? All right, I'm young. But how old does a girl have to be? How old was your mother when you were born?"

"Sixteen. Seventeen, maybe."

"I'll be eighteen in August." She turned away from him. "All right, go to Janice, then. She's older than I am. But she's not for you."

"She's a fine girl."

"Sure she is. One of the best. She'll make a good wife, but not for you."

Abruptly he turned away. He was a fool to start anything with this kid. Yet the feel of her in his arms was a disturbing memory.

"We'd better get back."

"All right . . . sure."

There was no more talking. Dodie Saxon strolled along through the snow, completely unconcerned. Yet Mabry was worried. She should be careful. No telling what could happen to a kid like that. There was fire in her. Plenty of it.

Outside the shelter she reached up to take the venison down, and as she turned away, carrying one haunch of it, she reached up with her bent forefinger and pushed it under his chin. "You big stiff," she said, and laughed at him.

He stared after her, half angry, half amused.

Tom Healy came out of the shelter. He whistled softly at the sight of the fresh meat.

"See any Sioux?"

"No. They're smarter than a white man. In bad weather they stay under cover."

"Don't blame 'em."

"Got a glimpse of the vans." He was tying the venison and rabbits to one end of a rope. "Burned down to the wheels."

He tossed the rope over a high branch and hauled the meat up into the tree, but well out from the trunk.

"How's Maggie?" he asked.

"Better," Healy said. "Ate a little solid food today, and she's breathing easier. Maybe it's the fresher air. Maybe it's the food. Anyway, she's better."

"Knew a trapper once, took sick 'way out in the brush all by himself. He just drank water and laid around eating berries and roots. Got well, too."

"She's a long way from well."

"We'll sit tight a couple of days, anyway."

Dodie looked out. "There's coffee on. I thought you'd want some."

He crawled into the shelter and accepted the cup Dodie handed him. Healy said something to Janice and she laughed. Healy's hand was on her arm. King Mabry looked at them over his cup, his face unreadable. Dodie glanced at him, then said, low-voiced, "Don't let it bother you. They've worked together a long time."

Mabry was startled. "Is it that plain?"

"Yes . . . and she feels the same way."

"You're wrong."

"No. I can see it. Only she won't admit it, even to herself. She won't admit she could be in love with a gun fighter."

"Don't blame her. It would be a dog's life, for a woman."

Dodie made no reply to that, only adding, "She's

Eastern. She doesn't understand. Not even after what happened."

"What about you? You seem to."

"I do."

It made sense, of course. And he was a fool even to give it a thought. Yet he was human. He wanted a home. He wanted to be loved and to love. Only there was no place for it in his life, not unless he could let it all be forgotten with the passing years. A few would try, and fewer would succeed. Yet it did happen.

What could he offer? He was a saddle bum, and every job offered would have to be examined like this last one, where what they were hiring was the gun, not the man. He would always have to guard against that.

Dodie sat across the fire from him, doubling her long legs under her. Looking at him brought a quiver of excitement to her. He was strong . . . very strong. Not alone with the muscular strength that came from hard work and harder living on the edge of the wilderness, but with a toughness of fiber that was like finely tempered steel and could give, but never break.

Janice was a fool. Tom Healy was all right. He was an easy-smiling Irishman, lovable and tough in his own way, in his own world. He was a man who could make any woman content . . . unless there was something that leaned to that hard strength and inner toughness, that needed it in a man.

Tom Healy was wonderful, but he was a tamed man. King Mabry was broncho stuff. He would never be tamed. Quiet, yes. Easygoing in his way, yes. But inwardly there was always that toughness of purpose, that leashed fury that could break loose as it had in the fight with Griffin at Hat Creek, and with the Indian. He had that indomitable something more important than mere prettiness or niceness.

Dodie picked up the gun that lay on the blanket beside her and handed it to Mabry. It was her father's gun.

The one he had carried through all his Western years.

"Where'd you get a gun like this?"

"It was my father's."

"Dead?"

"In Colorado. A fight over water rights."

"Was that your home?"

"Kansas, New Mexico, Colorado."

Thoughtfully he returned the Colt. She could see that he knew it was a good gun. The kind he himself might have carried.

## Chapter Fifteen

FOUR DAYS passed slowly, and there were no further signs of Indians. Mabry killed another sage hen, and through a hole in the ice he caught several fish.

Healy tried rigging his first snares, and on the third day he caught his first rabbit. He killed another one with a thrown stick while it struggled in the deep snow.

Once, scouting near the Hole-in-the-Wall, Mabry found the tracks of two shod horses coming northwest out of the Hole. They were riding into the rough country east of Red Fork, but what drew his greatest interest was the fact that, backtrailing them, he found they had scouted the opening of the Hole with great care. Evidently they had expected to find something or somebody there.

The tracks of one horse were familiar, but it was late that night before a reshuffling of the cards of memory returned it to consciousness. He had seen that same track at Hat Creek Station.

It had belonged to the horse ridden by Joe Noss. . . .

They had, he knew, stayed too long in one place. Yet it had been necessary to give Maggie a chance to recuperate. Another long ride without rest could be the end of her.

Returning on the fourth day, he found that a rider had followed his previous day's trail to a ridge overlooking the shelter. By now there were so many tracks that the shelter could easily be located.

There had been no sign of Barker and Boyle since they had left the wagons to find Healy and kill him. So far as appearances went, they had vanished into nothingness. The Indian attack had come, killing Wycoff and Griffin, but by this time Barker undoubtedly knew the girls were still alive, and that they, with the money, must now be with Mabry.

115

It was possible that they had now been joined by Joe Noss and his companion, who undoubtedly knew of some hideout in the Red Creek Canyon country, for, not finding anybody at the Hole, the two riders had headed northwest without any hesitation, obviously toward a known destination. It was probably at this destination that Barker and Boyle hid out following the destruction of the wagons.

The tracks that came to the top of the ridge had undoubtedly been left by one of this group. Hence it could be taken for granted that Barker now knew their exact location.

King Mabry thought this out as he rode down from the ridge after finding the tracks. It was time to move. Regardless of Maggie, they must go on.

When they had finished eating that night, he turned to her. "Feel up to riding on?"

"Any time," she assured him quietly.

"All right. We'll sleep four hours. Then we move."

"It'll still be dark," Healy said.

"Exactly. We'll have about three hours of travel in darkness, three hours of start on anybody who waits for daybreak. And unless I miss my guess, it will be snowing."

Maggie rode the black, bundled up in blankets and the buffalo robe. Dodie and Janice were to take turns on the Indian pony.

King Mabry led off at a fast walk. He headed upstream in a fast, sifting snow, and he held to a buffalo trail he had located several days before. After the snow wiped out the details, the tracks made by the buffaloes would offer them some means of hiding their trail.

Despite Maggie's weakness and the fact that none of the others was used to wilderness travel, Mabry held to a fast pace. At midmorning they stopped in a dense grove of pines, built a small fire, and had a hasty meal. When it was completed there was no rest allowed. Starting them on, Mabry remained behind with Janice to obliterate the remains of the fire.

"You're careful," Janice said. "Is it the Sioux?"

"Or Barker. Probably both."

They walked on in the steadily falling snow. The temperature was only a little below freezing now. It was a good time to travel, and Mabry gave them no rest. After three hours they paused for a hot bowl of soup, then pushed on, with Mabry scouting the country ahead and around.

Where they now rode, fuel was scarce and growing scarcer. Mabry was worried. Sensitive to every change in the weather, he knew they were in for another storm. The snow was increasing, and it was growing steadily colder. The little wood where they now rode would burn faster than a man could gather it. What they must find was a well-wooded stream, and quickly.

Somewhere on his left were the Nowood badlands, across Nowood Creek. The stream richly deserved the name it had been given a few years earlier.

He took Janice's arm. "See that tall, lightning-struck pine? On the point of the hill?"

"Yes."

"Take the lead. Tom will have to help Maggie. Head for that pine, then wait there for me. I'm going to take the pony and scout around."

Mabry started off at a swift gait along the ridge. The wind was picking up, and within a few minutes the snow was a curtain that shut them from his sight when he glanced back.

They walked on, moving slowly. Janice kept glancing ahead to watch the pine, but blowing snow made it ever more difficult. Sighting a queer, rocky formation on a hillside in line with the pine, she used that for a mark.

The older snow was crusted and would support their weight, but the black horse often broke through.

During a momentary halt, Janice glanced at Maggie. Her features were taut and gray when she removed the scarf from her face.

"Can you stick it out?" Healy asked.

"I'll be all right."

There was no sign of King Mabry.

Janice came up to the rock, and when they topped the hill above it she looked for the blasted pine. She could see nothing in any direction but blowing snow. It was very cold.

"Tom, we'd better stop here. I don't know whether we can go straight or not."

"You came straight to this rock? And it was lined up with the pine?"

"Yes."

He walked back in their tracks until he was a dozen yards from the rock. "Now you walk out this distance in line with the rock and me."

When he moved back to the rock he had Dodie go out ahead and line up with Janice and the rock. In this way they moved on, their progress only a little less rapid than before.

Suddenly Healy called out. Through the momentarily thinned snow he saw the blasted pine to their left, not thirty yards off.

As they drew abreast of it, Mabry materialized out of the snow. Then he led them down the gradual slope. At the bottom, among the trees, they saw the faint gleam of a fire.

Dodie took over the cooking when they reached the fire. Tom Healy began rustling wood, then noticed Mabry, who was scouting away from the fire, restless and uneasy.

"What's the matter, King?" Healy asked.

"I saw the tracks of four riders . . . shod horses."

Janice knew that if he had been alone, he could have got away or rode out and hunted them down and forced an issue. Tied to her and Dodie and Maggie, he could not do that. The initiative was left to Barker and his men.

Once they reached the Montana settlements, Barker was finished. The story would travel, and once it was told, someone was sure to remember that he had been associated with Henry Plummer.

They improvised a shelter and Maggie dropped off to sleep, exhausted by the long ride. Healy wandered in search of fuel, and Mabry squatted near the fire, close to Janice.

"You never look into a fire, King," she said curiously. "Don't you like to?"

"It isn't safe out here. A man should keep his eyes accustomed to darkness. If he suddenly leaves a fire after staring into it, he's blind . . . and maybe dead."

"Do you always think of things like that?"

He looked up at her, his eyes amused. "Sure. If I didn't I'd be buried somewhere."

The snow fell, covering their tracks, but making the new tracks they would make tomorrow even more obvious.

"What will you do now?" he asked suddenly. "You've lost your outfit."

"Start over, I guess. Tom will figure out something."

"Won't be easy."

"No."

"Town over in Montana. Coulson, they call it. About a year old, I think. You might start there."

Tom Healy came back with an armful of broken tree limbs and chunks from rotting logs. He stood warming his hands over the fire.

"Stage line from there to Virginia City, most likely," Mabry continued. "And from there you could go on west."

"And what will you do?"

"Hole up until spring. Then I'll ride into the Blues. Or over close to Bear Lake. I always liked that country."

Janice did not reply. She was remembering the long dusty rides in the vans or on the ill-equipped trains. The cheap hotels that were never without drafts, the cold dressing rooms.

"I'll run a few cows," he said, "and maybe some horses.

Horses do better in cold country. I could build myself a nice place . . . somewhere a man could sit and look a far ways. I want a good spring of water, cold and clear, and some trees."

"It sounds beautiful."

"Will be. Lonesome, though, for a man alone."

She saw Tom Healy turn away from the fire. He looked at King Mabry and there was no pleasure in his gaze. He was a man who felt animosity for no man. It was not in his nature, but she saw now that he was irritated. "You could always marry," he said bluntly. "Isn't that what you're building up to?"

Mabry had been chewing at a bit of stick as he talked. Now his jaws stopped chewing. For a long, slow moment he said nothing at all, and when he did speak his voice was low, and he looked from under his brows at Healy, who was still standing. "Yes, I could marry. Make a nice home for the right woman. That bother you, Tom?"

"Not if it isn't Janice," Tom said bluntly. "You offer no life for a woman."

"Tom!" Janice protested.

"No life for any decent woman," Tom persisted, "a life that would last until you put a bullet into somebody and had to go on the dodge again. Then what would become of your wife and this pretty little house with the view?"

King Mabry started to speak and then stopped. He got up and turned away from the fire.

Janice said quickly, "I can make up my own mind, Tom. And if King were to ask me, I'd say . . ." She hesitated. "I'd say yes."

Mabry turned back, looking startled. Tom Healy stared at her. His lips started to shape words, then stopped. His face was shocked and pale. Only Dodie showed no evidence of her feelings. She poked at the fire with a slender stick, one eyebrow lifted.

"And why not?" Maggie demanded belligerently. "Why not, Tom Healy? Is this any life for a girl like Janice? Let her have a home, some real happiness! And where could she find a better man?"

Healy stood right where he was. He looked sick, empty of feeling. After a while he said quietly, "I'll go to bed, King. You can have the first watch. Wake me when you're ready."

Taking his blanket roll, he went into the shelter.

King Mabry looked uncertainly around, helpless in the face of a totally unfamiliar situation.

"There's stew ready." Dodie's voice was practical. "Anybody want some?"

She dished up food for Maggie, then for the others. Neither Mabry nor Janice would look at the other, but they sat together on a log.

King Mabry was embarrassed. He wanted Janice Ryan. He wanted her as he wanted nothing else in this world, but he'd had no hopes of getting her. Nor had he any right to ask her to be his wife. He had been building to just that, yet even as he talked he was sure he would be refused. Once she had refused him, the foolish notion would be out of his mind; it would be all too evident how foolish he had been. When Dodie told him Janice loved him he had not believed it, not even for a minute.

He knew her attitude toward his kind of man. Nothing in her background had prepared her for him, or for the harsh terms of life on the frontier. She had the strength, the quality . . . that he recognized. Yet that she might accept either the life or himself he could not believe.

Now he groped for words and could find none, for he was a man without words, given to expressing himself in action, and the few words he used were those preliminary to action or associated with it. His philosophy did not come from books or religion, but from the hard facts of a hard life coupled with a strong sense of fair play, always linked with the realization that survival was for the strong.

Nothing in his adult experience prepared him for what he must do now. Afraid to look at Janice, afraid even to believe what had happened, he ate hungrily, as much to render himself incapable of speech as because of hunger.

Dodie alone seemed unexcited. He glanced at her, but her face was composed. Remembering the few minutes in the woods, he might have expected some reaction. Yet he knew better. Not from Dodie. Dodie was a soldier. She took things in stride and crossed her bridges when she came to them.

"Tom?" Dodie called. "You want to eat now?"

"Leave it by the fire."

Dodie put her hands on her hips and stared impudently at Janice and Mabry. "What *is* this? Why doesn't somebody kiss somebody? Are you two going to marry? Or are you scared, King?"

He looked up and growled at her. "I'm not scared. You . . . you talk too much!"

Dodie laughed. "But I don't *always* talk. Do I, King?"

He looked up at her, remembering the moment in the woods. It was in her eyes that she remembered, too, and was laughing at him.

"You go to bed!" he growled. "You're too smart!"

"Well," Dodie replied, "at least *I'd* know what to do."

King started fussing with the fire. He was guilty and embarrassed. For a few minutes he had been afraid Dodie would mention his kissing her. And then he realized she would not, she just wasn't the sort. In fact, she was pretty regular.

He tried to switch his thoughts to the problems of tomorrow, yet he was too sharply aware of the presence of Janice and that they were now alone.

He looked around at her finally. "Mean it?"

"Yes."

"It won't always be easy."

"Nothing is. At least, I'll have a home."

The word shook him. A home . . . He had not known a home since he was a child. But what kind of home could he offer her? A home where he might be brought in a wagon box any night? He had seen others taken home that way, some of them mighty good men. And he was asking Janice to share that.

King Mabry got to his feet. He felt he should do something, but he did not know what or how. He could not just walk over and take her in his arms. He picked up his rifle.

"Going down to the creek," he said.

He swore bitterly at himself as he walked away. Behind him, when he glanced back, the fire was tiny and alone. Janice sat where he had left her, staring into the flames.

Snow crunched under his feet, and he glanced at the sky, finding breaks in the clouds. Against the pale night sky the trees etched themselves in sharp silhouette. A star gleamed, then lost itself behind drifting clouds.

At the creek bank he stopped and rigged a snare, placing it in a rabbit run he had seen earlier. He needed no light. This he had done often enough to know every move. Out in the darkness a branch cracked in the cold, and some small animal struggled briefly and then was silent.

He had been a fool even to think of marriage to Janice. Now she would tie her life to his, and his destiny was tied to a gun. If they got out of this alive, there would be more trouble. And there was no assurance they would get out.

So far they had been fortunate. With the Indians they had been lucky, and only the fact that snow had come in time to blot out their trail had kept them alive. It was not his doing, although he had done his part, as had Healy. The real winner here was the very thing they were fighting now, the weather.

He listened into the night. There were only normal night sounds. On winter nights, if anyone moved within a great distance, it could often be heard. He shifted his rifle and turned back toward the campfire.

The fire had burned low, so he laid a foundation of sev-

eral chunks of similar size and length, then shifted the
coals to this new base and added fuel. When the fire was
burning well, he cleared the ground where the old fire had
been and unrolled his bed on the warm ground. It was an
old wilderness trick, used many times.

How many such nights had he spent? How many such
things had he learned?

Gloomily he walked to the horses and whispered to
them, rubbing their shoulders. The black stamped cheerfully.

He tried then to visualize the trail ahead, to plan what
could be done, and to put himself in Barker's place. Of
one thing he was positive. Andy Barker would come again.
He would not give up while there was still a chance, and
now he had three men to help.

After a rest, he took his rifle and scouted away from the
fire toward the creek that separated them from the Nowood badlands. At times he was as much as a quarter of a
mile out, but he saw nothing, heard nothing.

He was not relieved. Barker had to make his move. He
dared not let them get to Montana and the settlements
with their story. He must kill every one of them. And besides, there was that gold on the paint pony—or that
would again be on it in the morning.

Barker had taken a leaf from Plummer's book on that.
The leader of the Innocents always had tipsters to advise
him of gold shipments or sales of property. He knew when
men left the gold camps with money, and few of them
ever survived that knowledge. Somebody had tipped Barker
to the gold that Healy carried.

It could not be far to Coulson, perhaps less far to the
Fort. Tomorrow would be clear and they could get in a
good day's travel. And he would push hard, without re-
gard to anyone. It had to be that way. It would be cruel
for Maggie, but if Barker overtook them she would die,
anyway. He had to gamble with one life to save any of
them.

Once they reached the Fort, Janice could leave the

company and the two of them could find a place to wait until spring and a trip into the Blues.

It was no life for a young and pretty woman, carefully reared as Janice had obviously been. Yet she had come from good stock and many such had taken to the pioneer life with ease and skill. And he knew a thousand ways to make such a life easier. Nor was he broke. His hand touched the money belt at his waist. It was not much, but in this country it was a stake.

There were cattle in Oregon. He could buy a few, and there was game around, so they could live off the country if need be. He would avoid riding jobs for other outfits and the risk of running into somebody who knew his reputation. That reputation had been built from Uvalde to Cimarron, from Durango to Dodge and Abilene. But west of Cheyenne not many would know him.

Returning to camp, he built up the fire and awakened Healy. "All quiet. Doesn't seem to be anybody within miles. Let 'em rest until full daylight."

Yet scarcely an hour later he was awakened suddenly by Healy's hand on his shoulder.

"King?" Healy whispered. "Wake up! Something's wrong! The snow's melting."

Mabry lifted his head a little. He could hear the steady drip of snow melting from the trees, and feel the warm softness of the air. He lay back on his bed, smiling. "It's all right," he said. "It's the chinook."

"I couldn't figure what was happening."

"It's a warm wind, that's all. By morning there won't be a snowdrift in the country."

Mabry stretched out again, listening to the lulling sound of dripping water. They could travel faster now. And it would simplify the feed problem for their horses. The snow had been getting deep even for mountain-bred stock.

When he awakened the sun was shining in his eyes and the sky was wide and blue.

## Chapter Sixteen

BY KEEPING to the high ground where there was less run-off and so less mud, they made good time. The air was clear and they could see for a great distance. Nowhere was there any smoke, nor did they come upon the tracks of any party of horsemen.

Mabry scouted well in advance, studying the country. He knew all the signs, and watched for them, noticing the tracks of animals, grass bent down, and watching for any sudden change of direction in the tracks of animals he saw. Such a change might indicate the presence of men in the vicinity. At least, at the time the animal passed.

Yet by nightfall, when they came down off the hills to camp in a coulee, they had seen nothing, and had miles behind them. All were toughened to walking now.

It was Healy that saw the tracks first, the tracks of un-shod ponies. Healy spoke quickly, indicating them. A moment later, they saw the Indians.

The party was large, numbering at least twenty. Even as they were sighted, the Indians started walking their horses toward them.

"It's all right," Mabry said. "They're Shoshones."

They came on, spreading out a little as they drew near, the leader lifting his right hand, palm out. He was a wide-shouldered man with graying hair. As they came to-gether, he lowered his hand to grip Mabry's palm.

"Me High Bear. Friend to Gray Fox. You know Gray Fox?"

"Knew him in Arizona," Mabry said. Aside to the others, he added, "Gray Fox was the Indian name for General Crook."

Mabry glanced at the dozen spare horses they were driving with them. Those horses could be an answer to

eir greatest problem. The point was, would the Shoshones
ade? Yet he should know, he told himself, that an
ndian loves nothing better than a trade.

"Trade horses with the Crows?" he asked.

High Bear chuckled. "We trade. This time they know
." He glanced at the followers of Mabry. "Where you
orses?"

Mabry explained, taking his time and giving the story
s an Indian would tell it, in great detail and with many
estures. He told of the fight with the renegade Sioux on
ne Red Fork, and the flight of their party.

The story was more than a mere account. Mabry told
for a purpose, knowing well that the Shoshones were old
nemies of the Sioux, and that they would read the story
hemselves if any tracks remained. So he told the story of
neir flight, of the shelter and the sick woman. It was a
tory most Indians had themselves experienced, and they
stened with attention.

The story was also a prelude to a horse trade. The Sho-
hones, knowing they had fought enemies, would be more
villing in a trade now than they might have been other-
vise. The fight with the Sioux made them allies of a sort.

"Camp close by," High Bear said. "You come?"

Swinging in behind the Shoshones, they followed a half
nile down the coulee to a camp of a dozen lodges. Indian
hildren and dogs came running to meet them and to
tare with wide eyes at the strangers. Within a few minutes
hey were all seated around a fire, eating and talking.

King Mabry brought the spare weapons from the horses
nd laid them out neatly on a blanket near the fire. He
nade no reference to them, but managed an effective dis-
lay that drew immediate attention from the Shoshones.
The rifles were in good shape, but the handguns were old
nd much used.

The Shoshones cast many sidelong glances at the weap-
ns. Indians were always short of ammunition and rarely
ad rifles enough to go around. It was upon this that
Mabry was depending. If a trade could be arranged, they

might get horses enough to elude Barker and get to th
Montana settlements in quick time.

High Bear picked up the fine-looking Winchester 7
that had belonged to Griffin and turned it over in hi
hands. He obviously had a fighting man's appreciation o
a good weapon. "You swap?" he suggested.

"Maybe," Mabry admitted, without interest. "We coul
use three or four ponies."

High Bear continued to study the gun. That he like
the balance and feel of it was obvious. Mabry picked u
an older rifle and showed it to the Chief. "Two ponies,'
he said gravely.

The Shoshone did not even glance at the rifle, but con
tinued to examine the Winchester.

Mabry took out his tobacco sack and passed it around
High Bear rolled a smoke as quickly as any cow hand, bu
most of the Indians smoked pipes.

"That bay pony," Mabry said, "and the grulla. I migh
be interested in them."

High Bear put down the Winchester and picked up th
nearest handgun, an old Colt .44. "No good," he said. "N
shoot far."

Mabry reached for the gun. "Look." He gestured to
ward a pine cone thirty yards off. It was a big cone, wide
as a man's hand, and longer. As he spoke, he fired. The
pine cone split into many pieces.

"Waa-a-ah!" The awed Indians looked from the pine
cone to Mabry.

Mabry picked three pine cones from the ground near
the fire. "Throw 'em up," he said to Healy. "Throw 'em
high."

Healy tossed the cones into the air and Mabry blasted
the first two as they went up, then shifted the old gun to
his left hand, palmed his own gun, and fired. The cone
was dropping fast when the bullet struck. It shattered into
bits.

The Shoshones talked excitedly, staring at the gun. High

Bear took the Colt from Mabry and examined it. "You shoot fast," he admitted. "Gun shoot good."

He turned the weapon over in his hands. "Maybe all right. How much you want?"

For an hour they argued and protested, trading the guns from hand to hand. They shared the meal the Shoshones had prepared and Janice made coffee, which the Indians drank with gusto. Finally, after much argument, a deal was consummated.

In exchange for the Winchester 73, an old Spencer .50, and the worn-out Colt, they got three ponies. By distributing the packs among all the horses, none carried too much weight.

At daybreak, with a fresh supply of jerked meat traded from the Indians in exchange for extra ammunition and a blanket, they returned to the trail.

Healy rode up and joined King Mabry, who was once more riding the black. "That meat was mighty tender," he said, "and had a nice flavor. What was it?"

"Venison."

"I never tasted anything quite like it. How do they get it so tender?"

"Squaw chews it," Mabry replied matter-of-factly.

"*What?*" Healy searched Mabry's face for some indication that he might be joking, his sick expression betraying his own feelings. "You don't mean to tell me—"

"Sure," Mabry said. "Squaw chews the meat until it's tender. Then she cooks it. Never cared for the idea, myself."

High Bear had been interested in Mabry's account of the renegade Sioux, and promised to backtrack the party and see if they could be rounded up. Knowing the ancient enmity between the Shoshones and the Sioux, and considering the sizes of the two parties, Mabry was sure that if High Bear found the Sioux, that would be one party less to worry about. But High Bear assured him his party had come upon no tracks of white men or shod horses.

All the Shoshones in the party had been among those who had served with General Crook under Chief Washakie at the Battle of the Rosebud. They were friendly to the white men, and had been fine soldiers in that battle.

Riding steadily north under a sky as balmy as that of spring, they found little snow remaining except on the hillsides away from the sun. Nevertheless, Mabry was uneasy.

Yet despite his wariness, the quietness of the country, and the reassurance of the Shoshones, they almost walked into an ambush.

Tom Healy was riding point, with Mabry scouting off a hundred yards to the left, when the Indians struck without warning. Suddenly, with no previous indication of their presence, a half-dozen Indians arose from a ravine. Only Healy's shouted warning saved them.

Healy had been watching a bird, the only movement in all that vast sweep of land and sky, and he had seen it suddenly swoop for a landing in some brush at the ravine's edge. When it was about to land it fluttered wildly and shot up into the air again.

Healy shouted and swung his rifle one split second before the Indians stepped into view. Healy had fired as he swung the rifle, and his shot caught the first Indian in the chest. The Sioux screamed and grabbed at the brush to keep from falling.

Dodie, who was still carrying the shotgun, swung her horse and rode swiftly forward, firing first one barrel and then the other. Mabry came in at a dead run, sweeping wide around the rear of the little column to draw fire away from it. Reins upon the pommel, he sat bolt upright in the saddle, shooting fast into the scattered Indians.

Suddenly they were gone. Mabry swung his horse. Healy was on the ground, his arm through the loop of the reins, his rifle ready.

"Cover us," Mabry said as he swept by, and hurriedly he crowded the women over into a shallow dip in the hills away from the ravine.

How many Indians there were, he had no idea. At
least two were down, but he was sure there were more
Sioux than had revealed themselves, and that they were
in for a fight.

There was no adequate shelter, no place to fort up. Just
the hollow dip in the hills that was at least fifty yards
across and twice that long. Then he saw an old buffalo
wallow.

In a minute he had the three women on the ground in
the buffalo wallow and had led the horses to the lowest
part, where brush and high grass concealed them a little.
Yet he doubted the horses would be killed unless by a stray
bullet. The Sioux undoubtedly wanted the horses as much
as anything else.

Healy came in last and swung down. The surprise attack had failed utterly, largely because of Healy's alert-
ness. Even Janice had ridden out with an old pistol in
her hand.

Mabry glanced at her, but said nothing. Yet he looked
at Dodie thoughtfully. "You'll do to take along." he said
sincerely. "You put some shot into one of them."

Janice was putting the pistol back into its holster. For
an instant his eyes met hers and he smiled. "Another
minute and you might have killed an Indian," Mabry
said.

"They were attacking us," she said defensively.

"I know. That's the way it is."

There was a long time then of crouching in the sun in
the buffalo wallow. Wind stirred the tall grass, lazy white
clouds floated against the vast blue of the heavens. The
horses stamped and blew.

"They've gone," Janice said.

"No," Mabry said. "We'll wait."

A slow hour drew itself by on the canvas of the sky.
Mabry's shoulder was damp where it pressed against the
earth.

Three women, horses, weapons. . . . It was unlikely the
renegade Sioux would abandon the attack so quickly.

There was no rush. There was no warning of sound
only a faint whisper in the grass that was not the wind
and a sudden rifle barrel appearing on the ridge of the
hollow. Yet Mabry caught the gleam of sunlight even as
it appeared. He took a chance and held low against the
earth atop that low crest.

He squeezed off his shot even as the rifle muzzle swung
to bear on Healy. Mabry could see nothing but that
muzzle, but his shot struck with a sullen thud. A Sioux
lifted up, blood streaming down his face, then fell face
down over the lip of the hollow and lay sprawled out on
the grass.

At the same instant, bullets laced the hollow with dead-
ly fire. Healy replied, shooting fast three times.

And then again there was silence.

King Mabry wormed his way out of the buffalo wallow
and went up the slope to the dead Sioux. He retrieved his
rifle and a small pouch of ammunition, then edged up to
the hill. Looking through some grass, he peered over the
edge. Before him stretched a brown grassy hillside, empty
of life. The sun was bright and warm. The grass waved
idly in the light wind, and as far away as the distant line
of Nowood Creek, there was nothing.

He lay perfectly still, watching. His eyes searched the
ground to left and right. Then, rolling over, he drew back
a little and looked all around. He saw nothing. Yet the
Indians were there. He knew they were there. And with
each moment of delay, somewhere Barker was drawing
nearer.

In the buffalo wallow, almost concealed from where he
lay, were the others. And they had been too lucky. Too
beautifully, perfectly lucky. Since the killing of Guilford
and his own comparatively minor wounds, they had come
through unscathed, aided by their elusive action and the
weather.

Yet every hour increased the odds against them. The
law of averages would not let them escape forever, and
steadily the odds piled up.

Despite the warmth of the sun, the ground was cold. It ate into the hide, into the flesh and bone. It had lain under snow too long, was frozen deep, and the light air of the chinook could not touch the solid cold of the earth beneath them. Yet he waited, knowing well the patience of the Indian. An advantage, of course, was that these renegades were mostly young men, fiercely proud and resentful of the white man and eager to prove themselves as warriors. Dangerous as they might be, they were not so dangerous as seasoned warriors.

For a long time he saw nothing at all, then a faint movement. He lay still, watching, and he saw it again. They were coming up the slope, perhaps a dozen Indians. Yet this would not be the only attack. He slid back away from the rim and ran down the slope into the hollow. Quickly he explained.

From the east attack was impractical because of the bareness of the ground. The major attack would come from the bunch he had seen, but without doubt there would be a feint toward the horses from the other side.

"You stay with the horses," he told Janice. "Use your gun if they come at you. Tom," he turned on Healy, "you go up that slope. I doubt if you'll find more than two or three. Dodie will bring her shotgun and come with me."

Dodie took six shotgun shells from her pockets and put them on the ground near her. She looked white and strained, but determined.

He waited, his Winchester lying in the grass. Each of them had found a little hollow that offered protection.

"Remember," he said, "when they attack from the other side, *don't look around!* We'll have to trust to Tom to stop them. The moment you take in looking could be the one chance we'll get to stop them. And you're shooting downhill, so aim at their knees."

The minutes ticked by. There was no longer movement in the bottom. Mabry knew the Indians were moving up the slope in the grass, moving with the movement of the grass by the wind.

Suddenly a chorus of shrill yells rang out, then a shot, instantly followed by other shots.

Mabry was banking on the Sioux's believing he was still in the buffalo wallow. And he gambled right. Suddenly, with the sound of shooting, they came up and ran forward.

Dodie's shotgun lifted. "Hold it," he said quietly. "Let them come close."

They came on, trotting easily, confidently. They expected no trouble until they broke over the ridge. Mabry drew a deep breath and lifted his rifle. Behind them there was shooting now, intermittent fire. Healy was alive, then, and busy.

He could see streaks on a Sioux's body, and smudges of earth. The range was point-blank. He fired.

His bullet was aimed right at the Indian's beltline, and it seemed to knock the man's feet from under him. Instantly he moved and shot, hearing the smashing roar of the shotgun. He heard it once, twice, three times.

The attack broke and the Indians were running. He fired two more quick shots before they disappeared.

Dodie had reloaded and fired her third shot with scarcely a break.

He got to his feet. "All right, let's get back."

Janice was waiting, her face white and her gun in her hand. As they came up to her and to the horses, Mabry saw her looking up the opposite slope. Tom Healy lay there, unmoving.

Mabry stepped into the black's saddle and trotted the horse up the slope. As he swung down beside Healy, the Irishman looked up. His face was white and sick-looking, but he was uninjured. He got up slowly, stared wide-eyed at Mabry, and said, "Let's move, shall we?"

"Sure," Mabry said. "Get Maggie in the saddle."

Tom Healy walked away down the hill and Mabry waited for a moment, watching him go. Then he walked the few steps to the crest.

Two Indians lay sprawled on the grassy slope. One of

them was crawling away, dragging a broken leg. The other wasn't going to crawl anywhere again.

That Indian had come close, too close. Healy's bullet had struck the mechanism of the Sioux's rifle, smashed into jagged lead, and ricocheted, ripping the Sioux wide open. Part of the breech had been smashed by the bullet and sent flying upward, ripping the Indian's throat. It was a gruesome sight. No wonder Healy was sick.

King Mabry rode back down the hill and joined the little cavalcade. "We'll move now," he said, "while they're getting up nerve to try again or deciding to run."

He led them out, moving fast, going over the edge of the hollow to the west and keeping the hill behind them, into the bottom beyond. He turned south with it, then circled west and back to the north. Riding hard for twenty minutes, they then slowed to a walk, then rode hard for ten minutes and walked the horses again.

Into the maze of ravines and low hills they rode, putting distance between themselves and the Indians.

It was almost dusk when they sighted the cabin and the corrals. There was a barn, too, but there was no smoke, and no evidence of life except a few horses in the corrals.

Bone weary and sagging in their saddles, they came down the slope at a walk. Nothing moved but the horses. All else was deserted and still. But it was a cabin. And here someone had lived. Their journey was almost at an end.

Janice turned and looked back. She could scarcely remember Hat Creek, and the towns and theatres before that were vague and unreal in her mind.

Yet it was late dusk, and they were riding up to a home. It was over now, all over.

## Chapter Seventeen

It was a strongly built log house near the junction of two small streams. Another creek flowed into one of these above the confluence. There was a wide grassy space around the house, but on the streams there were dark rows of trees, and near the house a few huge old cottonwoods and a pine.

King Mabry's hail brought no response from the house, and they rode on into the yard. The earth was hard-packed, and the barns—mere sheds—showed recent use. And there were the horses in the corrals. Swinging down, Mabry loosened his gun in its holster and went up on the porch.

His moccasins only whispered on the boards. All was dark and still. Lifting his fist, he hesitated an instant, listening. Then he rapped, and the sound was loud in the clear night air.

He rapped again and harder, and only then did he see the square of white at the edge of the door. It was so near the color of the whitewashed door as to be almost invisible.

Leaning forward and straining his eyes in the dim light, he tried to read. Then he risked a match.

> Gone to Fort Custer. Rest, eat, leave wood in the box. No whisky in the house. No money, either. The whisky I drunk. The money I taken to buy more whisky.
>
> Windy Stuart

Mabry opened the door and stepped inside. He struck another match and, finding a candle, lighted it. The house was sparsely furnished, but there was fuel in the wood box and a fire laid on the hearth. The room in which he stood served as both living room and kitchen, and two curtained doorways led to small bedrooms, each containing two beds. Windy Stuart evidently often entertained travelers, and was prepared for them.

King Mabry put the candle down. He felt drained and whipped. His strength had been depleted by the loss of blood and the long rides. His wounds bothered him only because they itched, evidence that they were healing.

The house was clean and comfortable. It was too bad they could not stay, but must move on at daybreak. Yet Fort Custer could not be far away, and once they were there, their troubles would be over.

"Come on in," he called from the door. "I'll stable the horses."

"Got 'em," Healy replied. "You take it easy."

Mabry lifted Maggie from her horse and helped her into the house. When he put her down on one of Windy Stuart's beds, she looked up at him. "I'm beat," she said, "but I feel better."

He walked to the door, looking out into the night. There was a good field of fire except for those trees. Windy Stuart knew the danger of those trees, but probably hated to cut them down. I wouldn't, either, he decided.

Janice followed him to the door. "Don't be so restless. We're safe now," she told him.

"I was thinking about Barker."

"Forget him. That's over."

"No. He won't give up that easy. Some folks never give up."

"You're so right," Dodie said from within the house. "Some don't."

"But what can he do now?" Janice protested.

"His troubles really begin when we tell our story at Fort Custer, which looks like our first settlement. He may think we're dead, but I don't believe that. We left plenty of sign, and Barker struck me as a careful man. Besides, he has help now."

The moon was rising and the cottonwoods looked stark and bare in the vague light. The barn cast its shadow, and the bare white poles of the corral looked like skeleton bones in the moonlight. Out in the stable a horse stamped and blew.

Over the trees, somewhere in the meadow beyond the streams, a wolf howled.

"You're borrowing trouble, King. They'd be afraid to attempt anything now."

He did not argue, yet King Mabry had that old, uneasy feeling. The woods out there were dark, but they did not feel empty, and the hunted man learns to trust his senses. On too many occasions they had saved his life.

Inside it was warm and cheerful. Carefully he hung blankets over all the windows. Old Windy had been well provided for here, and evidently got along with the Crows, whose country this was. The Crows were friendly, anyway, and, like the Shoshones, were old rivals of the Sioux.

Soon a big fire blazed in the fireplace and Janice was busy preparing a meal while Dodie was setting places at the table.

Tom Healy dug out his razor and shaved, combing his hair carefully. Somewhere among the things brought from the wagons he found a clean shirt.

Not to be outdone, Mabry shaved. When he belted on his guns again, he went out through the back door and scouted around in the dark. It was quiet . . . too quiet.

How far away Fort Custer was, he had no idea. But Barker would know, for this was his old hunting ground. And Barker would know the lay of the land, so he could choose his own spot and time.

It was a quiet supper. Several attempts to start a conversation died at birth. King Mabry had his ears alert for sounds, and Tom Healy seemed sour and unhappy. Janice was curiously quiet, looking long at King from time to time. Only Dodie seemed gay. She laughed and chattered for a while, but then even she was silent.

After supper Mabry went outside and Janice followed

him. Together they walked out under the big old cotton-woods.

"King," she said, "there must be no more killing. No more at all."

"A man does what he has to do."

"I couldn't marry you if you did."

It was the old story, and it stirred a deep-seated irritation within him. As if he went hunting for men to kill.

"You've no right to say that, Janice. Who knows what will happen in the next few days? I don't want to kill, but I have no desire to be killed, either."

"You can avoid it."

"Perhaps. . . . You've never tried to avoid a gun fight. You have no experience with which to judge a man like me."

"If you kill," she protested, "you're no better than they."

"What about the war? You told me your father was in it."

"That's different."

"Is it? Because they carried flags? This is war, too, a war to see who will hold the West—those who come to build homes or those who come to grab and steal."

Janice shook her head. "It isn't right, King. It just isn't right."

Miserably he stared at the mountains. How could he make her understand? Or anyone who had not been through it? They tried to judge a wild, untamed country by the standards of elm-bordered streets and convention-bordered lives.

"What about the Indians? Should I have let them kill us?"

"They were Indians."

"But they're men too. Often good men in their way. The Indian is fighting for a way of life as good for them as our way is for us."

She was silent but he knew she was unconvinced. She hated the gun he wore, hated the thought of what it had done, and even more of what it might do. In Virginia men who killed had been hung or sent to prison, and she could see no difference here.

He could guess her thoughts and searched his mind for arguments, but he was not a man of words, and none would offer themselves now. He sensed the rising strangeness between them, and sought desperately for something to sweep it away.

He reached out for her and drew her to him, but there was a stiffness in her back, and no willingness. She was coming to him, but she had yielded nothing.

She looked up at him. "Promise me you won't use your gun again."

He dropped his hands from her arms and drew back a little. "I'd be a fool to make such a promise. This is a land of guns."

Angrily she turned away from him. "I think what they say of you is true! You *like* to kill!" Then she added, "And you don't love me. If you did, you'd do what I want!"

"No," he replied quietly, "I wouldn't. To do what you want would be no proof of love. I'm my own man. I have to live my life as it comes to me, according to my own conscience."

"*Conscience!*" she flared. "You don't know the meaning of the word!"

Turning abruptly, she went inside. Helplessly he walked back to the porch and stood there in the darkness. Why had he not promised and ended the argument? There was a good chance they would never see Barker again. Yet he knew, even as the thought came to him, that he could make no such promise. He hoped never to use a gun again, yet if the time came when it was necessary, use it he would.

He remained where he was until the fire inside was down to coals and all were in bed but himself, and even then he hesitated, for the old restlessness was upon him. The soft wind still blew, only more lightly now, and somewhere out under the sky a lone wolf howled at the moon, and the echoes gave back their answer from the strong-walled cliffs, and sounded again and again from the crags and shoulders of the mountain.

He stepped down from the porch and walked around the corrals, soft-footed as a big cat. On the porch again, standing in the darkness, he rolled a last cigarette, then lit it in carefully cupped hands.

"Janice . . . Janice . . ." He whispered the name softly into the darkness.

And the darkness gave back no answer. Only the wolf howled again, and the long wind whispered down the ranges.

# Chapter Eighteen

At DAYLIGHT King Mabry rolled out of his bed and dressed quickly. Healy was already up and puttering about in the outer room. Mabry heard wood splintering, then the crackle of flames. As he stamped his feet into his boots he heard the door slam and knew Healy had gone out.

Mabry swung his gun belt around his lean hips and buckled it. He flipped his gun lightly, as was his habit, to make sure it was free in its holster.

Walking into the outer room, he poured water into a basin and bathed. The wash bench outside the door was too cold for these winter mornings.

When he had his hair combed, he crossed to the fire and added a few sticks, then poured coffee. Janice was up and dressed, and when she heard him moving she came to the door and spoke to him.

The coffee was fresh, hot, and strong. He took his cup in his hand and walked to the door. Healy was nowhere in sight, evidently in the barn feeding the horses.

Janice poured a cup and joined him at the table. She looked fresh, competent, and lovely, much as she had seemed at Hat Creek when he first saw her. "I'm sorry, King. Really sorry. But you wouldn't have me go against what I believe, would you?"

"Better have some coffee." He indicated the cup she held.

Dodie came from the bedroom, and a few minutes later Maggie emerged, walking carefully, but under her own power. She was thinner, but her eyes were bright.

"Never let it be said," Mabry commented, "that the Irish aren't tough."

"I'll make it," Maggie replied grimly. "I'll make it yet."

Janice looked across the table at Mabry, who avoided her eyes. The room was growing warm and the smell of coffee was pleasant. Outside there was frost on the ground, and frost atop the corral bars. In here it was cozy and warm.

Maggie looked around, and when she spoke her tone held a touch of wistfulness. "It's a nice place. A woman could do a lot with it. And those trees! I always loved big old trees."

"In the spring," Mabry said, "the hills are green. The peaks over there always have a little snow, but down here the meadows are soft and the cattle walk knee-deep in grass."

"And I'll be walking the boards of some dusty stage," Maggie said, "and dressing in a stuffy little dressing room."

"You'd never want to do anything else, Maggie," Dodie said. "If you had a home like this, someday you'd smell grease paint or hear a spatter of applause and you'd be gone again."

"Maybe . . . maybe. But I'd still like to try it."

Mabry finished his coffee cup and put wood on the fire. He knew there were things to be said. Janice was wanting to say them or expecting him to say them, and he felt like doing anything but talking.

"Where's Tom?" Dodie asked suddenly.

"Outside. Feeding the horses, most likely."

King walked to the window and glanced out. The sandstone hills were bleak and frosty this morning. Only here and there was there any snow, lying in white streaks in crevices where the sun never reached. He walked back to the table and, putting down his cup, rolled a smoke.

Janice went twice to the window to look out, and the second time Mabry glanced up, meeting her eyes. "Where is he?" she asked. "I'm hungry."

"I'll fix something for him now," Dodie said. "We'd all better eat if we're going to get an early start."

Dodie took the frying pan and put in some grease. There was bacon, and she found some eggs. She held one aloft. "I never expected *these!* I was beginning to think nobody ate anything out here but beef and beans!"

Janice got to her feet. "I want some fresh air. I'll go help Tom."

She went out quickly, drawing the door shut behind her. Grease sputtered in the frying pan. Mabry watched Dodie breaking eggs and slicing bacon. "Don't let it get you, King," Dodie said. "She'll change."

He glanced at her, but made no reply. The smell of bacon frying was making him hungrier. He drew deep on his cigarette and sat back in the buffalo-hide chair, liking the warm feeling of the house, the sound of the fire, the comfortable sounds of a woman moving about.

Even a place like this . . . just so a man could call it home. What did it get a man to be forever wandering? He saw a lot of country, and he learned a lot, but what was the use of that unless it could be passed on to somebody?

He remembered when he was a youngster, fresh to the plains, remembered the call of distance, the challenge of strange valleys, of canyons up which no man had gone, of far heights and the lonely places of the desert.

He had wanted it all then, he had hoped never to stop. He had loved the smell of lonely campfires, the crisp feeling of awakening on a frosty morning, even the smell of the buffalo-chip fires. He remembered seeing thousands upon thousands of buffaloes, each with frost on its shaggy shoulders and head. He remembered the creaking of the saddle and the challenge of a distant rider. . . .

That was for a man when he was feeling the first sap of youth in him. It was good to keep some of it always, as he would, but there was a time when any man worth his salt wanted a wife and a home and a son.

Gloomily he got to his feet and walked across the room. A man had to put roots down, to build something, not to be just a restless drifter with a saddle and a blanket roll.

A man needed something to call his own, something to work at and constantly improve. What was a life worth if it was wasted in idle drifting? Sure, a man had to see the world. He had to look at the far horizons, he had to see the lights of strange towns; he had to measure his strength with the strength of other men.

Beyond a certain age a drifting man was like a lost dog, and had much the same look about him.

Maybe he was a fool not to listen to Janice. After all, they might never see Barker again, and in the Blues or near Bear Lake a man might lose himself. There were a lot of Mormons down that way, and mostly they were a peace-loving lot. If he stopped wearing a gun, or wearing it in sight, then he might never have to use it.

"Better sit up to the table," Dodie said. "I'll start some more bacon." She walked to the window. "That's odd," she said. "I don't see anybody."

"Probably in the barn."

"All this time? Anyway, there's hardly room in that little place for—" She broke off sharply. "King, something's wrong out there!"

He put down his fork, his mouth full of eggs and bacon. Getting to his feet, he walked toward her, but stopped well back from the window, where he could see out without being seen. "Now what's the trouble?"

"There was a rabbit," Dodie was whispering. "He started past the cottonwood over by the corrals. Then suddenly he bolted right back this way!"

Mabry studied the situation. No rabbit would be frightened by anything out there unless it was a man.

He had been telling himself to put aside that gun too soon. Dodie was right. There was something wrong. Healy and Janice had been gone too long and there was nothing for them to do in the barn. Scarcely room to move around with those horses in there.

"You stay here. I'll go out back."

"They'd be watching the back, too. I know they would."

Dodie walked to the rifles against the wall. She picked one up and moved the shotgun nearer the door. "I can help, King. I can try."

"Stay out of sight." As he spoke, he was thinking it out. They could have been out there waiting. They must have been, or Janice and Tom would be back by now. They were holding the two of them and waiting for him to come out.

Suddenly he remembered the root cellar under the house. There was an outside entrance, too. And on the side of the house nearest the barn.

He opened the cellar door, lifting it up from the floor. "You sit tight. Hold the house and don't let anybody in."

Softly, on light-stepping feet, he went down the steps. At the bottom he paused to study the situation.

The cellar was under the whole house. There were several bins of vegetables and a crib of corn. There were also several hams and slabs of bacon. A dozen feet from the foot of the steps was the cellar door to the outside, and luckily, it was standing open. Windy Stuart had been careless, but his carelessness might save all their lives. Opening that door would have made noise.

Between the barn and the cellar door was the woodpile. The end of the barn was toward him. He studied it with care, then returned to the steps and went up into the house until his head cleared the floor.

"Dodie, you count to a slow fifty. When you get to fifty, open the door and then pull it shut. Don't by any chance get in front of that door. Just open and close it, but make some noise."

"All right."

He went back down the steps and crossed to the outside door. He mounted those steps until his eyes were at ground level. Some scattered wood offered slight protection. He went up another step. There was nothing in sight.

The end of the barn looked solid. Having seen the care with which Windy Stuart had built, he doubted if there was so much as a chink through which wind might blow or an eye might look.

Gun in hand, he waited. He had a moment then of standing with his mouth dry, a moment when he knew that in the next instant he might clear those steps and feel the smash of a bullet, feel it tearing through his vitals.

It was only the fool or the witless that felt no fear. What a man must do was go on, anyway. Suppose he went back into the house and waited for them to move? He knew what they would do. They would wait just so long, then tell him to come out or they would kill Healy and Janice.

Now the move was his . . . and you did not win by sitting on your hands. Long since he had learned the only way to win any kind of fight was by attack, attack always with whatever you had.

The door slammed.

He sprang into the open and crossed to the shelter of the barn's end in swift strides. He flattened himself there, listening.

Silence, and no sound within. Then a horse stamped.

Before him, in the open place in front of the house, he could see nothing. He could see some of the trees, but only a corner of the corrals.

There was probably a man inside with the prisoners, and another at the corrals. Yet if he was guessing right, and there were four, where were the other two?

Barker, Art Boyle, Joe Noss, and the fourth man who might be Benton. The man who had ridden through the Hole with Joe Noss.

Two in the barn, maybe. That was more likely. One with the prisoners, and one with a poised gun, to . . .

Where could the other be?

If he had come this far without attracting a shot, the fourth man must be where Mabry could not see him, or he Mabry. Considering that, he decided the fourth man must be in front of the house, between the cottonwoods and the trail.

From that point he could cover the front door, but he must also have seen Dodie's hand when she opened and closed the door. So he might have guessed that their plan was not working.

A boot scraped. Then Healy called out, "King? Can you come out here a minute?"

"Louder!" King heard Barker's voice. "If you make one try at warning him, I'll kill her!"

"King!" Healy yelled. "Can you come out?"

There was a period of waiting, and Mabry heard a muffled curse. "No use." It was Art Boyle's voice. "They're wise. That girl's got a rifle."

It was time to move. Time to move now, before they did. They had numbers, so it was up to him to catch them off stride. There was such a thing as reaction time. That instant of hesitation between realization and accomplishment. It was upon this that he must gamble.

There was little cover behind the trees, and it was cover only from the front, not from the flanks. Boyle had yelled from in front of the house when he had seen the rifle in Dodie's hands. Mabry darted out quickly, not quite past the front of the barn, but enough for Boyle to see him.

Boyle saw him and started to swing the rifle. He was too slow. Mabry's gun was breast-high and he glanced along the barrel as he fired.

There was an instant when time seemed to stand still. Mabry saw the man's white, strained face. He saw the rifle swinging, and he stood perfectly still and cold, with no heat in him, and pointed the gun as he would a finger. The pistol leaped in his hand.

The teamster's rifle was coming up when Mabry's bullet smashed him in the teeth. His head jerked back as if slammed by a mighty fist, and he fell. Then he rolled over, clawing toward the fallen gun, but blood gushed from his mouth and he stiffened out.

Mabry flattened himself back against the wall of the

og barn, gun up, ready for a chopping shot. Boyle rolled over, choking on his own blood, and lay still.

From within the barn there was absolute silence.

One gone . . . three to go. One at the corral's end and at least one in the barn, probably two. He thought of that and realized his advantage, if such it could be called. Four people in close quarters, two of them ready to shoot, but neither of them wanting to kill Janice, neither wanting to kill his partner. They would have one target, he would have two; they would be separated and his two friends would undoubtedly be shoved back against the wall or in a corner.

He remembered seeing Dodie's shadow as she moved within the house. He remembered thinking that the sun was up, shining through the gray clouds like a poached egg in a pan of gray grease. He remembered hearing a wind rustle the cottonwood leaves. His gun was up and he was going in. He was going into two blasting guns, but he had the advantage of being the only one who knew just when he was going in.

He tried to recall the inside of the barn he had seen but once. He tried to figure just where they would be. One of them was close against the wall near the opening. That would be Barker.

There had to be one there. It was the logical place, as near the door as possible. And it was not a narrow door, but half the width of the barn front.

When he went in he could not get a shot at that man. That fellow would be too far over on his right, unless he managed to swing close enough and fire from against his body. But if he figured right, the prisoners would be in the corner behind Barker, and if he shot Barker the bullet might go all the way through and kill one of them.

He would have to take the other man first. He would have to nail him quick and fast, then drop and fire at Barker.

"You can't make it, King!" Barker shouted suddenly.

"We've got you! Come out and drop your gun or we start killing!"

They didn't know where he was, then. Not from the sound of that order. They didn't know he was so close. Or he did not think they did.

Throwing down his gun would be no use at all. They were out to clean the slate by killing them all. But there was that item of reaction time. And it was always better to attack than to wait.

His mouth was dry and his heart pounding. He wiped his palm dry on his shirt front, then gripped his gun. And then with a lunge he went around the corner and into the barn.

Outside a rifle smashed sound into the morning an instant before a bullet whipped past him.

He sprang through the door and into the barn. He saw Joe Noss first and fired as his feet flattened out. Noss had his gun up, but Mabry had calculated every move of his turn, and as his left foot landed solidly, he fired from directly in front of his body.

Mabry's bullet caught Noss alongside the second button up from his belt, and Mabry had a confused realization that Healy had lunged forward, knocking Barker off balance. Noss's shot went into the roof as he fell backward into a sitting position.

Barker had grabbed Janice for a shield and she was struggling to free herself. Suddenly Barker thrust her hard against Mabry and sprang through the door as Healy missed a wild grab at him.

Healy swung and grasped the gun from Noss's hand as Barker tore free, but before Healy could get through the door, Mabry grabbed him.

"Hold it! There's a man outside who'll cut you down!"

King Mabry motioned Healy back. There were two desperate men out there who knew that not only fifteen thousand dollars, but their own lives turned on the issue of the next few minutes.

He grabbed the tie rope of the black and swung the

big horse. The smell of blood had excited the animal, and he was trembling. Throwing a leg over his back, Indian style, Mabry gave a piercing yell and Healy slapped the horse across the haunches with his hat.

With a lunge, the black horse broke from the barn. A shot rang out, and then Mabry fired, shooting under the horse's neck. Then he pulled himself to a sitting position on the horse as he saw Barker break for cover.

Slamming his heels into the black and yelling like a Comanche, Mabry started after him. Something jerked hard at his shirt collar and a gunshot slammed from somewhere near. He saw from the tail of his eye a man spring from cover near the corral and run for his horse. Bullets from Healy's gun were dusting the ground around him.

Barker turned as he ran and tried to brake himself to a stop. He tried to bring his gun up fast, but it went off into the ground as the black hit him with a shoulder that knocked him reeling.

Mabry swung the horse so short the animal reared as he turned and Barker fired from his knee. The bullet laid a hot lash along Mabry's cheek, and then King Mabry fired three times as fast as he could slip the hammer off his thumb.

Barker backed up, swearing. He swung his gun around as Mabry dropped from the horse to the ground. There was a spreading stain on Barker's shirt.

Mabry held his fire, waiting in cold silence as the wounded man struggled to lift his gun. Outside the barn Healy and Janice stood, frozen in silence. On the steps of the house Dodie held her Winchester, halfway to her shoulder.

Barker's gun came up, then the muzzle tilted down and Barker's eyes glazed over. He took two bent-kneed strides on legs no longer able to hold his weight. Then he crumpled to the hard-packed earth and the gun slid from his hand.

King Mabry waited, his eyes cold, taking no chances. Barker's body heaved at the waist, then slowly relaxed.

Mabry began to eject shells from his gun and to reload.

Only a solitary bullet had remained in his gun. As he loaded up there was absolute silence. He was conscious then of the cottonwood leaves whispering in the cool morning air. He was conscious that his cheek stung and that otherwise he was unwounded.

Once more he had come through. How many breaks could a man get?

He walked to where his other gun had fallen from his waistband when he hit the ground. He picked it up, remembering to be glad that he always carried six shells in his guns . . . no problem in the Smith and Wesson. There was a faint trickle of blood down his cheek.

The wind rattled the cottonwood leaves and his hair blew in the wind.

Janice was staring at him, her eyes wide, her face white. He started toward her, but when he was within three strides of her she turned suddenly and walked away toward the house.

"She's upset," Healy said. "It's been a tryin' thing."

"She'll be all right, King." Maggie had come out to them, walking carefully. "She owes you plenty. We all do."

King Mabry's eyes were gray and cold. "Nobody owes me anything, Maggie. You'll be all right now. You go on to Fort Custer."

"Aren't you coming?"

"Maybe later."

Dodie grounded the butt of her Winchester. "Give her time, King. She's Eastern."

Bleakly he looked at her, then turned away. He walked to the black horse and caught up the halter rope.

## Chapter Nineteen

LIGHTS from windows cut into the darkness of Wallace Street, where dwindling crowds drifted homeward.

Here and there the boardwalks echoed to the boots of walking men, or they splashed through the mud in the streets toward the few spots that remained open. Down by the eating house several horses stood three-legged at the hitch rails and somewhere a pump rattled and water gushed into a tin pail.

Tom Healy lighted his pipe and looked down the street. Janice should be dressed by now. They would get something to eat and return to the Five Story Hotel, which was their home in Virginia City.

This had been their last day in town, the last of a successful week.

He drew on his pipe, walked a few steps, and came back to lean against an awning post. A drunken miner stared at him, muttered something under his breath, and went on by, steering an erratic course down the muddy street. Healy glanced up the street, hearing the sound of a horse's hoofs, some late rider coming in off the trail.

He looked, then slowly straightened away from the post, his breath going out of him. The big man on the black horse wore a black hat, pulled low, and a short sheepskin coat, and there was no mistaking him. It was King Mabry.

Healy took the pipe from his mouth, feeling sick and empty. He stared at the pipe.

So Mabry was back. This he had feared.

King Mabry had mounted and ridden away from Windy Stuart's ranch without a backward glance. And later that day they had started on for Fort Custer.

At Fort Custer they had found Maguire. He was putting

153

on a show there, and when he had accepted his money and heard their story, he quickly offered to stake them to a fresh start. They had played Fort Custer themselves, then Butte, and now here. It had been but three weeks since the gun battle at the horse ranch.

Yet that gun battle was already the stuff of legend. Windy Stuart's name was no accident, and he had returned in time to help bury the bodies. He looked over the ground and heard the account of the fight, and rode with them to Fort Custer, refusing to allow this, the best of all stories, to be told only by others.

Nobody had seen Mabry. Where he had gone nobody knew. He had ridden from the horse ranch into oblivion, vanishing until now. Yet no night had come that Healy had not thought of what would happen when he did come.

Janice said nothing at all. She played her parts and sang as always. She was quiet, even less inclined to talk, always anxious to get back to the hotel after the theatre. Nothing in her manner or in what she said gave Healy any clue to what she was thinking or feeling.

King Mabry walked his horse to the tie rail before a saloon, dismounted, tied the horse, and went inside. If he had seen Healy, he gave no sign. He was wearing a gun.

Tom Healy knocked out his pipe against an awning post. The theatre was across the street from the saloon, and from the window Mabry would be able to watch the door of the theatre. Tom Healy put his pipe in his pocket. A man had to know. He had to know these things, once and for all.

During the past week he and Janice had drawn closer together. Nothing had been said, but there seemed to be an understanding between them.

Healy crossed the street and pushed open the door of the saloon. King Mabry was standing at the bar, his hat shoved back on his head, a glass in his hand. He looked bigger and tougher than ever.

Four men played cards nearby. Two men stood at the bar. Healy stepped up to the bar near Mabry.

"A little o' the Irish," he said.

Mabry glanced at him as Healy took the bottle and filled his glass. Then Healy shoved the bottle along the bar. "Has the smell o' the bogs," he said. "Try it."

"Thanks."

Mabry filled his glass. "Luck," he said, lifting it.

Healy hesitated, then smiled slightly. "Why, yes. Luck to you!"

They drank and Healy put his glass carefully on the bar. "She's across the street, King. She'll be coming out any minute."

Mabry turned toward him. "You love her, don't you?"

"I'd be a liar if I said no."

"Then why tell me?"

"You're a good man, King. A mighty good man. Maybe your luck is better than mine. But a man has to know, doesn't he, now?"

"He does."

The door across the street opened and Janice came out, looking up and down the street.

"She's looking for you, Tom."

"But maybe she hopes to see you."

"No," King Mabry said, "it's you, Tom. It's you she's looking for."

Tom Healy stood very still and straight, looking at Mabry. Then he held out his hand. "Good-by, King."

"Adiós."

They shook hands and Tom Healy went out the door and across the street.

Janice's hands went out to him. "Tom!" She kissed him lightly. "I was afraid you had run off with some other girl."

"In this town?" He tucked her hand under his arm. "Wait until we get to San Francisco."

"Can we get some soup? I'm hungry!"

"Sure."

Behind them a door closed. Healy heard boot heels on the boardwalk. Then he heard the sound of saddle leather creaking as a stirrup took weight, and a horse turning in the muddy street.

He opened the door of the café and Janice went in ahead of him. Healy glanced back up the street. The big man on the black horse, vaguely outlined in the shadowed street, was watching them. As they stepped inside, Healy thought the horse started forward.

They sat down, Janice's back to the window. As Tom seated himself, he saw a rider pass the window, walking his horse. For an instant the light caught him, showing only a bit of the saddle, a man's leg with a gun tied down, and the glistening black flank of a horse. Then he heard the horse break into a trot and he sat holding the menu, his heart beating heavily as he listened to the retreating sound.

He glanced at the grease-stained menu. And then the door opened. Healy felt his stomach go hollow and he looked up.

It was Dodie.

She glanced quickly around the café. "Which of you owns that sorrel outside?"

A cow hand looked up. "I do, ma'am."

"What's your price?"

He hesitated, then grinned. "For you, only thirty dollars."

Swiftly she counted out the money. Then she turned to Healy. She glanced from Janice back to him. "Tom, I—"

"I know," he said.

She turned quickly and went out the door, and a moment later a second rider passed the window, and the horse broke into a run, a dead run from a standing start.

Light showed on the saddle and a shapely leg, the horse's flank glistened, and then the sound of pounding hoofs faded gradually away.

"Hey!" The cowpuncher turned a startled face. "She took my saddle!"

"It's all right," Healy said. "I'll buy you a new one."

Then Tom Healy looked down at the menu. "It's onion soup," he said. "They only have one kind."